Tell me a Story

edited by Elizabeth Cooper

Hamlyn
London · New York · Sydney · Toronto

Contents

This book belongs to

Kerry Macdonald
41 Fraser Road
Dingwall

illustrated by John Speirs

Some of the stories in this book first appeared in storybooks published by the Hamlyn Publishing Group in 1959, 1960 and 1961.

Other stories were specially written for the book by Elizabeth Cooper.

Published 1978 by The Hamlyn Publishing Group Limited
London · New York · Sydney · Toronto
Astronaut House, Feltham, Middlesex, England
© Copyright 1978 by the Hamlyn Publishing Group Limited

ISBN 0 600 38765 8

Printed in Great Britain

A house that became a home

A long time ago, there was a house that liked to be lived in. But although it had a garden full of honeysuckle and roses, and a doormat with WELCOME written on it, and a board by the gate which said TO LET, nobody wanted it.

'What a pity,' sighed the little house. 'I'm sure I would make a good home for someone.'

Now, one autumn day, a fat old toad hopped across the doormat and said, 'I suppose you have no cosy corners to spare?'

'Goodness me,' laughed the house that liked to be lived in. 'I'm full of corners. Take your pick.'

So the toad chose a corner under the back doorstep, and settled down. The house that liked to be lived in thought a toad was better than nothing.

Then, one rainy day, the little house saw a mouse running up the path looking for shelter.

'Come inside,' called the little house. 'You'll get wet.'

'Thank you,' said the mouse, slipping in through the space under the front door. 'You are a nice house.'

'You can stay for as long as you like,' said the house that liked to be lived in. 'There's plenty of room.'

'Can I really?' said the mouse. 'Then I think I will. I have noticed a good place in your sitting-room where I could gnaw a hole.'

So the mouse moved in, and the little house could hear her scampering round all night long.

One day, the house that liked to be lived in heard a strange buzzing noise which grew louder and louder as it came nearer. It was a swarm of bees flying into the garden, to try the honeysuckle and roses.

'Mmmmmmm, honey,' they buzzed. 'What a beautiful garden! Mmmmmm. Would you mind if we lived in your roof?' they asked the little house. 'We would like to be near such beautiful flowers!'

'Not at all,' said the house that liked to be lived in.

The bees buzzed all round the roof until they found a hole the right size for them. They crept in and built their honeycomb as fast as they could.

One spring day, a pair of swallows flew onto the board by the gate which said TO LET.

'This house would do very well,' they said to each other. 'Would you mind if we built a nest, little house?'

'Oh, I should like that,' cried the little house, who loved baby birds. 'Only you must be careful not to disturb the bees.'

The swallows chose the wall under the eaves by the bedroom window, and all day long the house that liked to be lived in watched them. They flew back and forth with straw and mud to build their nest.

One stormy night, the wind blew and blew and it blew so hard that in the morning the little house found out that the board by the gate which said TO LET had blown away.

'I don't mind. I don't need it now,' laughed the house that liked to be lived in. 'I have the nicest lot of tenants a house could wish for.'

Tim Hare's party invitations

In a few days' time it would be Tim Hare's birthday, and he was busy writing invitation cards. Each card had neat printing and dotted lines, like this:

...... invites ......
...... to his party on ......
......

On the first dotted line he wrote his own name, and on the second line he wrote the name of the person he wanted to ask to his party. On the last line of all he wrote 'Saturday'.

Tim had a bright idea and said to Mrs Hare, 'I had better put "Please answer soon", on each card, then we shall know how many icecreams to buy, won't we Mummy?'

That Monday morning, Tim took all the cards to the woodland post office.

'What a lot of letters!' said Mr Badger the post master. 'Is there one for me?'

'There is, Mr Badger,' said Tim, shyly, 'but I'm not going to *give* it to you. It must be posted with the rest because it's a surprise.'

When Wednesday morning came, and nothing had arrived in the post, Tim hurried to the post office.

'Please, Mr Badger, are you coming to my party?' he asked.

Mr Badger smiled mysteriously, and said, 'I can't tell you that, Tim. You see, I haven't posted my answer to your invitation yet, so how could I know?'

Poor Tim Hare! He hadn't the heart to ask anyone else whether they were coming to his party or not, so he went off home.

It was nearly tea-time that afternoon, when a shiny red van drew up outside Hare Cottage and Tim's friend Sam Squirrel the postman came in with a big, bulging mailbag.

Tim took the mailbag inside and for the rest of the afternoon, he and Mrs Hare were busy counting the answers to his invitations. EVERYONE was coming to Tim's party. What a lot of icecreams Mrs Hare would have to order!

Camping indoors is fun

John and his sister Jenny watched the rain run down the window, and said to their mother, 'Oh dear, it's raining and we did want to go out and play at camping in the woods.'

'I know you did, my dears, but you must wait until the rain stops,' said their mother.

'What can we do while we wait for the rain to stop?' asked John and Jenny, staring sadly through the window.

'I'm going to clear some of the rubbish out of the attic this morning. Would you like to come and help me?' asked their mother.

'Oh yes please, Mummy,' said John and Jenny, and they followed her up the stairs.

Soon all three of them were busy sorting through the old junk in the attic. John stopped when he saw a big white dust sheet covering a chair in the corner.

'Mummy, can we borrow that sheet?' he asked.

'Of course you can,' she replied.

Later that morning, John and Jenny ran downstairs with the sheet and found two tall chairs which they put a little way apart. Then they hung the big sheet over the top of the chairs, and it made a perfect tent for them.

So they were able to play at camping after all that day, and they didn't take any notice of the rain beating down outside. In fact, they decided it was much more fun than camping in the woods.

A blue ribbon for Magellan

Annabel was so proud of Magellan, her pet mynah bird, that when her school's annual pet show came round, she decided to enter him as well as Leonard the labrador.

It was hard filling out the entry form because there were so many classes to choose from, but Annabel had some help from Magellan. She read them out while he sat and listened.

'"Most Obedient Pet", "Most Colourful Pet", "Most Unusual Pet"...'

'That's it, that's the one,' called Magellan excitedly. 'The "Most Unusual Pet" class is exactly right for me. And Leonard can enter for the "Most Obedient Pet".'

The day finally came.

The "Most Obedient Pet" class was judged first and Leonard was delighted to be declared the winner.

It was Magellan's turn next, so he and Annabel went into the ring.

The judge looked at all the other animals first. He finally reached Magellan and was just about to open his mouth to speak, when there came an announcement in a loud voice that sounded just like his: 'And now I am pleased to award first prize to this magnificent mynah bird.'

Annabel gasped, 'Oh Magellan, what *have* you done?'

But the judge roared with laughter and said, 'I can see why he's such an unusual pet. He shall indeed have the blue ribbon,' and he tied it around Magellan's neck.

Magellan was very pleased.

Read more stories about Magellan on pages 42, 67 and 82.

opened, a hand came in and Dozy and the letters were scooped into a large sack.

'Help!' squeaked Dozy.

Just then, the village policeman came riding along on his bicycle and got off to speak to the postman who had collected the letters. The sack was rather heavy so the postman put it down on the ground. Out of the opening tumbled Dozy and the little dormouse streaked off up the lane to the woods and safety.

'I'm afraid the letter-box wouldn't suit us,' said Mrs Dormouse when she heard Dozy's story. 'But never mind, I've found a beautiful place under the roots of a beech tree.'

Then, to cheer him up, she added, 'But you are very brave, Dozy. Never before have I heard of a dormouse who posted himself in a letter-box!'

Dozy and the red letter-box

'Winter will soon be here,' said Mrs Dormouse. 'It's time I started searching for a good place to make our winter nest.'

'Please can we help?' squeaked the little dormice.

'Very well,' said Mrs Dormouse. 'But don't go too far.'

Dozy, the youngest of the dormouse family, thought, 'How surprised they'd all be if I found the best place of all.' And then he scampered off up the lane.

The first thing he saw was a red letter-box. It was screwed to a wooden post at the side of the road. He ran up the post and popped through the letter opening.

At the bottom was a fat bed of letters which would make a very cosy nest.

Who-o-o-o-sh! Suddenly, a handful of letters shot through the opening onto his head. Poor Dozy was buried in them.

Then the front of the letter-box

But next day, when the twins went to look at their pond, they got quite a surprise. Right in the middle of their lovely pond sat Chickadiddy the big, fat hen.

'Why, I do believe she is laying an egg in our pond,' laughed Paul. And so she was. All the water had soaked away and the sun had dried out the sand. It made a perfect nest for Chickadiddy, but it was not a very good pond for tadpoles.

'I've heard of duck ponds,' laughed Patrick, 'but we've made a chicken pond! Would you believe it?'

'A chicken pond, a chicken pond, we've made a chicken pond!' sang Paul.

So the tadpoles are still in their big glass jar and each day Chickadiddy lays an egg in the pond. She thinks it was made specially for her, and neither Patrick nor Paul will ever tell that it was once meant for something quite, quite different.

Chickadiddy's nest

The twins had decided to make a pond for their tadpoles which had been living in a glass jar since the day they were caught. So Patrick and Paul dug a hole in the earthy bank by their house and covered the bottom with sand from the stream. Then they put big white stones all round the edge, so that when the tadpoles turned into little frogs they would have cool caves to hide in. And between the stones they planted tufts of grass.

'Now I will fetch the water to fill it up,' said Patrick, going off with his bucket. But the water stirred up the sand on the bottom and made the pond very muddy.

'We had better not put the tadpoles in till tomorrow,' said Paul. 'It will have cleared again by then.'

Daffodil's smart new hat

Daffodil was a small grey donkey who gave rides to boys and girls at the beach.

'Phew!' she panted one day. 'It's hot. I wish I had some sunglasses to wear. But,' she added, 'I don't suppose they would hook onto me because my ears are in the wrong place.'

Then she saw a lady sitting holding a sunshade over her head.

'Now that's a better idea! I would love a sunshade. Only,' she added, 'I do need all my feet for walking, so perhaps it isn't such a good idea after all.'

Then, along came a young girl wearing a big, floppy, straw hat with a large, red poppy in the front.

'That's the thing for me–a sunhat,' cried Daffodil, jingling her harness.

Just then, a sudden gust of wind caught the girl's hat and blew it way up high into the air. It went over the top of a shelter, down into the road straight under the wheels of a car, then across the road to Daffodil.

Daffodil put one foot on the hat and stopped it.

'Oh dear,' panted the lady. 'Thank you so much for saving my hat.' She picked it up. 'Dear me, it's much too bent for me to wear now. I wonder where the nearest dustbin is?'

'Hey!' cried Daffodil with a toss of her head. 'Don't throw it away.'

Suddenly the young lady had an idea. 'I know,' she smiled, 'I'll give it to this little grey donkey.'

So she put it on Daffodil's head.

The little donkey hee-hawed her thanks. 'I'm the happiest donkey in the world now,' she said.

Daffodil was delighted. What a smart hat – the very thing to keep the sun off!

Bessie's rainbow quilt

There were seven piles of knitting wool neatly set out in a circle on the living-room floor. Bessie sat in the middle looking at the colours.

They were lovely and bright, she thought – red like a rosy apple, orange like a flame, yellow like the sun, green like grass, blue like the sky, deep purple like the ink in her new fountain pen and violet like the pretty little flowers in her garden.

'It's too hard,' declared Bessie. 'I can't decide what colour to knit my quilt. I like them all.' And she went over to the window seat to have a good long think.

It had been raining outside and now the sun was peeping through the clouds.

'Here comes the sun,' thought Bessie, as the warm rays shone through the window. 'Perhaps it will help me make up my mind. Red, orange, yellow, green . . . oh, I don't know.'

She looked out of the window and there, shimmering in the sky, was the most beautiful rainbow she had ever seen.

She counted up the colours – *seven*.

She said their names aloud – *red, orange, yellow, green, blue, indigo* and *violet* .

'A rainbow! Of course – my quilt will be all the colours of the rainbow.'

And she picked up her needles and her red wool and started knitting.

Benny Bear builds a house

Benny Bear was building a house. He was fixing the upstairs window frame when Andy Giraffe called to him, 'Benny, I'm having trouble with my car.'

'I'll fix it,' said Benny, coming down the ladder. He soon put things right and Andy thanked him very much. 'One day I'll do as much for you,' said Andy.

'It was nothing,' said Benny, and he went up the ladder and started on the window frame again.

'Benny,' called Henry Elephant, 'I'm having trouble with my new bike.'

'I'll fix it,' said Benny, and he came down the ladder. He soon found the trouble and put it right.

'Thanks, very much,' said Henry. 'If you ever want a bit of help let me know.'

'It was nothing,' said Benny and he climbed up the ladder again.

'There you are,' cried Olivia Ostrich. 'Do you think you could fix my lawn mower?'

'Of course,' said Benny and he went over to Olivia's house.

'That's very clever of you,' said Olivia when he had fixed the mower. 'Maybe one day I can do something for you.'

'Maybe,' laughed Benny as he climbed the ladder, but suddenly – BUMP – BER – UMP – BUMP – Benny slipped and tumbled from the ladder.

'Gosh,' said Benny, 'my wrist hurts,' so Olivia took him along to Doctor Kangaroo, who said it was sprained and bandaged it up.

Benny was worried and as he walked home, he thought, 'What am I going to do about my house?' But when he turned the corner he had such a surprise. Andy and Henry and Olivia were all working on the new house. The window frame was fixed and some of the tiles were already in place on the roof.

What good friends he had. They were paying him back for all the good turns he'd done them.

The silver brooch

Jackdaw loved pretty, sparkling things.

On Monday he flew right through an open window and stole a pretty necklace from a lady's dressing table.

On Tuesday he fluttered into a draper's shop through the open door and stole a card of coloured buttons.

'I wonder what I shall find on Wednesday,' thought Jackdaw as he gazed proudly at the treasures in his nest.

Well, on Wednesday he was very lucky. As he was flying through the wood his sharp eyes caught sight of something gleaming in the sunshine on the bank of a stream. He flew down eagerly. It was a beautiful silver brooch.

'I wonder who it belongs to,' said Jackdaw, as he hurried home with the brooch in his beak.

That very evening who should knock at Jackdaw's door but Mr Woodpecker. He frowned deeply and shook his head when he saw all the treasure.

'That's stealing,' he said sternly.

Jackdaw felt very ashamed. 'I – I didn't know it was wrong,' he murmured. 'I will take everything back, honestly I will!'

And he did, but he had no idea what to do with the brooch which he had found on the green bank.

As he was flying about, wondering what to do about it, he noticed a little girl kneeling down among the primroses. She was looking about anxiously.

Jackdaw guessed at once what the matter was. Holding the silver brooch tightly in his beak, he flew down and hovered right over the little girl's head. Then he let go and the brooch fell at her feet!

'Thank you, thank you, kind bird,' she cried happily.

And Jackdaw didn't mind that he had no treasure left. He was just pleased that he had made someone happy.

The red shoes

Nancy sighed as she tried on yet another pair of shoes in yet another shoe shop. 'I don't like any of these,' she grumbled.

'Never mind, dear,' said her mother. 'We'll find a nice pair somewhere.' And they walked on until they came to a funny old shoe shop called 'The Cobblers'.

Nancy's eyes opened wide, for there in the window was a wonderful pair of bright red shoes. She tried them on. They fitted perfectly, and as she stood in front of the mirror, her feet did a little dance. 'That's funny,' she thought, 'it's like magic, almost as if these shoes had a mind of their own.'

Bright and early next morning, Nancy put on the red shoes and, *skippity skip, hoppity hop*, they were on their way, out of the house and off down the road.

'Where are you taking me?' Nancy cried, but the shoes kept on going – through the grass in the park, along the river, over a bridge, and on and on . . . until, at last, they stopped, *in 'The Cobblers' shoe shop* .

'Well I never, they're back,' said the shopkeeper. 'There must be magic in those shoes, young lady.'

'A little too much for me,' gasped Nancy, out of breath. 'I think they've come back to stay.' And she took off the shoes and gave them to the shopkeeper.

He found another pair of red shoes for her – quite ordinary red shoes – and put the magic pair back in the window.

As Nancy walked out, she saw another little girl pointing at the shoes in the window, and she very nearly told her about their magic. 'But no,' she thought. 'I'll let her find out for herself.' And she smiled a very secret smile.

Chief owl Edward

Edward Owl was very worried about his first forest meeting. He had just been made chief owl of the forest, and it was his job to help the other animals with their problems. Now owls are known for their wisdom, but poor Edward wasn't at all wise.

'Oh, well, perhaps the questions will be easy ones,' he sighed as he settled himself in the oak tree. 'First question please.'

A rabbit raised his paw. 'Please, wise owl, can you tell us where the best carrots can be found?'

Edward thought hard. 'Er, I'm not sure—but I'll find out and tell you next Wednesday.'

'I want to know *now*,' said the rabbit crossly.

'Next question,' asked Edward feeling rather silly.

'How far is it from our forest to Nutworth Village?' asked a mole in a very serious voice.

'Well . . . I should say . . . er . . . about an hour on foot?' guessed Edward.

'An hour!' squeaked a squirrel. 'It's certainly not more than fifteen minutes.'

The group of animals started squeaking excitedly. 'He doesn't know. He's a wise owl and he doesn't know.' The little squirrels began to laugh at poor Edward. And the meeting was called to an end.

Soon Edward was left alone in the moonlight in his oak tree feeling very unhappy. At least, he thought he was alone until he noticed a squeaking coming from the grass below him. Peering down he saw a tiny field-mouse who said 'I don't want to ask you a question. I want to help you.'

'Help *me*?' hooted Edward amazed.

'Yes,' said the mouse. 'You see, mice aren't usually very clever, but I'm exceptional.'

'Er—what?' Edward gulped.

'Unusual,' explained the mouse. 'I can't help it. I love reading and learning and I'd like to teach the forest animals but I'm so tiny they'd laugh at me.'

'Yes, I expect they would,' said Edward. 'But I'm sure you could help me. Why, you could sit in the tree, hidden under my wing, and whisper the answers to me.'

The following Wednesday, Edward and his field-mouse friend met under the oak tree. They settled on a high branch and the field-mouse snuggled out of sight under Edward's wing.

Soon the forest animals were gathered around the foot of the tree.

'How long would it take to get to Whitestone Farm from here?' grunted the old mole.

Edward pretended to think but he was really listening to the little field-mouse.

'One hour and two minutes crawling, and thirty minutes at a scamper,' said Edward loudly.

The mole was pleased with the answer.

'I have a homework problem,' said a small rabbit. 'If a rabbit has eight carrots, and his sister takes away three and he gives his brother one, how many has he left?'

'Four,' said Edward.

The forest animals clapped their paws delightedly. 'Thank you, thank you, wise owl. We'll see you next Wednesday.' And they scampered away.

When they had gone the field-mouse crept out. 'I enjoyed that,' he squeaked.

'You were wonderful,' said Edward. 'Will you come and help me every week?'

'Of course,' said the field-mouse.

And he always did. So you see no-one ever found out that Edward the wise owl wasn't really wise.

Andy's wish comes true

'Do you know what I wish for most of all in the world, Mum,' said Andy before he went to sleep one night.

'No, tell me, what do you wish for most in the world?' asked his mother.

'A paintbox with all the colours of the rainbow in it,' sighed Andy, 'but it will take ages to save up the money for one.'

'You'll have your paintbox one day, dear, you'll see,' said his mother.

And Andy fell asleep dreaming about his paintbox full of rainbow colours.

When he came home from school the next day, there was somebody to see him – his granny. She gave him a hug and then she said, 'I found a rainbow when I was out shopping today, and I brought it here specially for you.' And she held out a big red box.

'What can it be?' said Andy.

And then, as he lifted the lid, he knew what she meant, for inside were rows and rows of paints in rainbow colours.

Andy couldn't believe his eyes. His very own rainbow paintbox! But how did Granny know that he wanted one?

He looked at his mother, and his mother looked at Granny, and Granny's eyes sparkled as she said, very simply, 'Wish on a rainbow, Andy, and your wish just may come true.'

A funny present for Porky

It was Porky Piglet's birthday and he was having a party. There were lots of guests. His sister was there, and three of his cousins. His two favourite aunties came, and quite a number of friends from school, including Ursula. Porky liked Ursula–she was his best friend.

She was the last to arrive at the party, and she handed Porky his present very shyly. 'Thank you so much, Ursula,' he said. 'May I open it now?'

'Yes, please do,' she said. 'It's nothing much, but I thought you would like it.'

Porky opened the little parcel. Inside was a small, stiff pink doll. He was puzzled. It seemed rather a funny sort of present to give a boy.

Next came the birthday tea–there were jellies and blancmanges, and fancy cakes and chocolate biscuits–and afterwards they played games until it was time to go home.

But Porky was rather quiet all the time because he was thinking about Ursula's present. It seemed such a funny thing to give him, and what was he to do with it?

Next day, he showed the doll to his mother, saying, 'This is what Ursula gave me, Mummy. But what do I do with it?'

'Oh, Porky, you're pretending! You know quite well what to do with it!'

But he didn't.

'I say, Tibby,' he said to the farm cat, 'do you like my present?'

'All right, I suppose,' she replied, 'if you like playing with dolls.'

'It doesn't seem to be for playing with, Tibby,' said Porky. 'Can you suggest something else it might be for?'

'I thought dolls were always for playing with.' And she crept away to look for mice.

Just then, Porky saw Ursula skipping gaily up to him.

'Hello, Porky,' she said. 'Have you eaten your sugar doll yet?'

Of course, *that* was it!

'No, Ursula,' he replied, 'but I have it in my pocket if you would like to share it with me.'

And they ate the sugar doll together.

Frankie the red fire engine sped up the hill to Gorse Common. He was on his way to see Gipsy Joe, whose wrinkled old face always lit up with pleasure when he heard the purr of the engine.

But today something was wrong. Joe's face was gloomy as he hobbled down his caravan steps.

'They've gone,' he cried. 'My donkeys are lost.'

'Oh how dreadful!' said Frankie. He knew that Joe loved his three playful little donkeys, Meeny, Miney and Mo.

'Perhaps they've just wandered into the town,' he suggested. 'Would you like me to search for them?'

'That I would,' the gipsy said.

'Don't worry,' called Frankie, and he raced down the hill.

'I had better try the market first,' he thought to himself.

He didn't know that, as he passed the vegetable stall, a bunch of carrots tangled itself on the last rung of his ladder.

In High Street, people began to point at Frankie.

'Look!' they whispered. 'Look who is following him.'

'Why are they pointing?' Frankie said

to himself as he turned into Main Street.

'Look!' the people whispered again. 'There are two of them now, trying to catch him up.'

As Frankie turned into North Street, the people all stopped and laughed, and Frankie began to feel annoyed.

'There are three of them now,' the people chuckled.

Frankie looked sternly ahead as he sped through South Street.

Three of them! And Frankie doesn't know!' the people chuckled.

As Frankie toiled up the hill to Gorse Common, Old Joe hobbled to meet him, and Frankie could hardly bear to tell him that the search had failed.

'I tried very hard. I am sorry,' he said.

'Sorry?' said Old Joe. 'Look behind you, Frankie.'

Frankie turned around to look.

'Goodness!' he gasped. For there, behind him, were three donkeys, Meeny, Miney and Mo!

'So that's why the people laughed,' said Frankie. 'I was looking for your little grey donkeys, and they were following me all the time.'

'Following the carrots,' said Old Gipsy Joe. 'What a way to catch a donkey!' And they both laughed.

Frankie the fire engine has another adventure on page 55.

Simon's clever hiding-place

The children were just about to begin another game of hide-and-seek in the garden when Uncle John appeared at the kitchen door.

'Come along, Alice,' he called. 'It's time we were starting for home.'

Alice had been spending two weeks with her cousins, Charles, Caroline and Simon, because her mother had been ill. But Mother was better now, and her father had come in his big, green car to take her home.

'Oh, *please*, Daddy! Can we play just *one* more game?' she begged.

'Well, just one,' he agreed.

The children cheered.

'It's Caroline's turn to find us,' said Charles, who was the eldest.

Caroline turned her face to the wall and began to count.

'Come on, Simon. I'll find a place for you to hide,' Alice said kindly.

Simon was only just five, and he couldn't usually find a place to hide. But this time he shook his head firmly.

'I've thought of a lovely hiding-place,' he said. 'And I don't want *anyone* to see where I go.'

'All right,' laughed Alice.

When they were out of sight Simon hurried to his hiding-place. It was warm there, and dark.

'If Caroline doesn't find me soon,' he thought after a few minutes, 'I will probably go to sleep.'

It didn't take Caroline long to find Charles and Alice, but she couldn't find Simon anywhere. Charles and Alice began to search for him, too, while Uncle John looked anxiously at his watch.

'I can't wait any longer,' he said at last. 'I want to be home before nightfall, and we have a long way to go. You'll have to say goodbye to Simon for us.'

So he and Alice climbed into the car, waved goodbye and drove off down the road.

'Now to find Simon,' said Charles, but though they searched high and low they couldn't find him anywhere.

They began to call, 'Simon! You can come out now. The game's over.' But Simon didn't appear.

At tea-time they called, 'Simon! Tea's ready.' Still he didn't come.

'Where can he be?' said their mother, beginning to look worried.

'Leave him,' smiled their father. 'He'll soon come out when he knows we aren't looking for him any more.'

But when there was still no sign of Simon at bedtime they all felt worried.

Then the telephone rang, and their father hurried to answer it. The others heard him laughing, then he put the receiver down and came into the living-room.

'We've found Simon!' he announced.

'Where?' they all asked.

'He hid himself in Uncle John's car,' their father told them. 'He crawled underneath a rug on the back seat and fell asleep. He didn't wake up until they reached home. That was Uncle John on the telephone and he says he can't possibly bring Simon back until next weekend.'

All the family laughed and laughed.

'Well,' Charles chuckled, 'that's the best hiding-place Simon's ever found!'

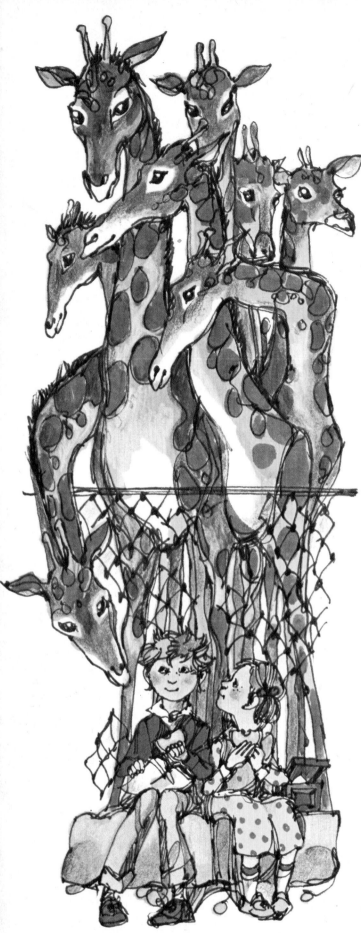

Lunch in the giraffe house

'Isn't it a lovely sunny day, yak,' called Joey to the big shaggy animal munching away on lunch in his enclosure.

'Mm, maybe,' grunted the yak, who was much more interested in his food than the weather. 'But I'd watch those clouds if I were you. I feel a little rain coming on.'

'Rain?' exclaimed Lizzie, Joey's sister. 'It couldn't possibly rain.'

'Rain?' said Daddy. 'Who said anything about rain? It's a perfect day to be at the zoo. Now you two, let's see if we can find the giraffes, and then we'll see about some lunch.'

'Ooh yes, a picnic on the lawn,' cried Joey, running ahead.

The giraffes were all inside their tall, red brick house, so Lizzie and Joey and Daddy went in too.

'Oh my, your heads are nearly touching the ceiling,' said Lizzie, staring up at the giraffes. There were eight long necks swaying above her like trees in the wind.

But suddenly, they heard something, a pitter-patter first, then a heavy drumming, and they knew it was rain on the roof. Oh dear, that was the end of their picnic on the lawn.

'What was that about a picnic?' asked a friendly keeper, who came in just then with some food for the giraffes. 'You can have your lunch in here where it's nice and dry. The giraffes won't mind.'

And they didn't. In fact, they enjoyed having Lizzie and Joey and Daddy to lunch in their house.

That sort of thing didn't happen very often!

The King's hiccups

The Palace Doctors were there, the Prime Minister was there, and even the Court Magician was there.

The King had hiccups.

'Another spoonful of the blue medicine, Your Majesty,' suggested one of the doctors.

'No, *hic*, no, *hic*, thank you,' cried the King angrily.

The Queen waved the Magician nearer. 'Try a little more magic,' she said.

So the magician got a bowl of water, and balanced it on the King's head.

'Now, close your eyes and put your arms out straight please,' he said to the King.

The King did as he was told.

Then the magician placed a stick across the King's outstretched arms.

The King looked very funny. '*Hic, hic, hic,*' he went, and the water spilt over the bowl and down his neck.

The magician raised his wand . . .

Then the Palace door flew open and the Court Jester tumbled through! He did a somersault, tripped over the carpet and landed PLOP, in the King's lap.

The bowl of water toppled over, and landed on the Jester's head. The stick flew into the air, and came down on the Queen's nose.

'You clumsy fellow,' shouted the King, 'this is no time for jokes. The Magician was doing some magic for my hiccups.'

'Bbbbbbbbbut, Your Majesty,' said the Queen. 'Your hiccups–they've gone!'

'So they have,' smiled the King. You shall have a reward, Jester.'

The Jester was amazed. 'Thank you Your Majesty,' he gasped.

'Away with the rest of you,' commanded the King. 'Next time I have the hiccups I shall know exactly what to do. No more blue medicine and magic for me,' he said thankfully, as he relaxed on his throne. 'Just send me the Jester!'

A big problem for Trumps

Trumps the toucan lived in a rather quiet corner of the zoo where he shouldn't have been bothered by people too much. But he *was* bothered, because every person who came up to his cage said something about his beak. Like the silly little boy who called out, 'A beak like that would make anyone fall off his perch.' Then, the smartly dressed lady who exclaimed, 'My goodness, that nose of yours must be a dreadful nuisance!' And the old man who warned him that he must be very careful it he wasn't to trip over his beak.

'Oh dear,' sighed Trumps after a particularly tiresome day, full of silly people saying things about his beak. 'I wish I weren't the only one with a big nose,' and he felt very sorry for himself.

But the next day, he didn't have time to feel sorry for himself. He spent the morning moving house to a lovely new cage right in the centre of the zoo where there were lots of other animals all around. And joy oh joy, Trumps noticed that all of them had big noses – the anteater, the elephant, the pelican, the tapir, the stork and the crocodile.

And from that day on, Trumps never took any notice of silly people saying silly things about his beak.

'It's a perfectly good beak,' declared Trumps, and all his new animal friends agreed.

Paddy's little yellow car

In a little cottage on top of Windmill Hill lived the brothers, Paddy, Peter and Nicky.

One soft summer evening, Peter and Nicky sat in their garden watching the sun sink behind the hills. They were waiting for Paddy who had gone to fetch the milk for their supper.

Then chugging up the hill, in a cloud of dust and smoke, came a little yellow car.

'It's Farmer Finch's car, Daphne,' said Peter. 'Perhaps Farmer Finch is coming to call on us.'

Sure enough, the car stopped with a groan and a hiccup, just outside the gate. But it wasn't Farmer Finch; it was Paddy sitting behind the wheel.

'What are you doing in Farmer Finch's car?' asked Nicky in surprise.

'It's mine now,' laughed Paddy. 'Farmer Finch has a new car and he was going to give this to his piglets to play with. So I bought it.'

'How lovely!' said Peter. 'What fun we shall have with her!'

'Tomorrow,' said Paddy proudly, 'I shall take you to the seaside for the day.'

'Hurrah!' shouted Nicky and Peter.

Very early next morning, they set off for the seaside and after an hour's drive they came to a crossroads.

'Where's the map?' asked Paddy, stopping the car, but Nicky had left it at home.

'Never mind,' said Paddy cheerfully. 'I think I know the way,' and, bumpity-bump, off they went again.

Soon they stopped for a picnic in a meadow with cool trees beside a sparkling brook and after lunch they lay down in the shade and went fast asleep. It was Paddy who woke up first.

'Someone's in the car,' he shouted, and they saw four little faces peeping over Daphne's bonnet.

'It's Farmer Finch's piglets!' said Nicky in surprise.

Suddenly Peter began to laugh and laugh. 'Oh dear, oh dear,' he gasped. 'This is Farmer Finch's field. Paddy has taken us in a big circle and we are nearly home again.'

'Bless my buttons!' roared Paddy. 'So we are.'

'Never mind,' giggled Nicky, 'we've had a jolly day. We'll go to the sea tomorrow – but this time we'll take a map!'

The cheeky monkey

Cheeko was a monkey with soft, brown fur and bright eyes, and he lived in a jungle far, far away across the sea.

Cheeko had a fine time swinging about in the tree tops: *swish, swish, swish*. He chattered to the other monkeys and the brightly coloured parrots–but he teased them as well. He was full of mischief, although he didn't really mean to be unkind.

In a clearing in the jungle there was a big pool, and in the evenings lots of animals came to drink from it. Rajah the elephant was one of these. He lumbered along slowly, swinging his trunk from side to side, and *splish splosh*, he would walk into the water.

Cheeko used to hide in the trees and wait for Rajah to come along, then drop coconuts on his head. This made Rajah very angry and he roared at Cheeko, 'You cheeky young monkey, I'll teach you a lesson one of these days.'

One evening, Cheeko sat waiting in a tree with his coconut. Lots of animals came to the pool to drink–zebras and antelopes, and many others. But Rajah didn't come.

Cheeko couldn't understand it. He twittered away to himself at the top of the tree, waiting until it was quite dark, and he could hardly see. He became very sleepy and his head began to nod . . .

The next time he opened his eyes all the stars were out, and so was the moon. Suddenly, he heard a rustling noise, and he saw Rajah down below limping along slowly. Something was wrong with one of his front feet.

Cheeko didn't throw his coconut this time. He swung down, *swish, swish, swish*,

through the branches, and followed Rajah to the pool.

'What's the matter?' Cheeko asked him.

'Go away if you have only come to tease me,' cried Rajah angrily. And *splish splosh, splish splosh*, he waded into the pool to drink.

Cheeko went and hid behind a bush and chattered anxiously to himself.

Rajah kept squirting water from his trunk into his mouth, but he was much too tired to bother about having a bath. Then *splish splosh, splish splosh*, he waded out again. The poor fellow seemed worn out, and with a groan he sank down to have a rest.

Cheeko peeped out from his hiding-place. After a while Rajah began to snore loudly, and the monkey knew he was asleep. He crept closer and closer, until he could have a look at Rajah's swollen foot. There was a big, sharp thorn in it. The little monkey managed to grasp the thorn in his tiny fingers. He gave a sharp tug, and it was out.

With a cry of rage and pain Rajah awoke and grabbed Cheeko with his trunk.

'I'll teach you to play tricks,' he shouted angrily.

Cheeko was frightened. 'I was only pulling the thorn out of your foot,' he cried.

The elephant held him in mid-air for a moment. He tried stamping his foot gently. Then he smiled, put Cheeko down and said he was very sorry.

'My foot feels a lot better,' he said gratefully. 'Thank you, Cheeko, you are a good little fellow.'

After that they were the best of friends and Cheeko never played naughty tricks on Rajah again.

The leap-frog race

Wizzy and Wozzy were two little frogs who lived in the pond in the park.

One day, as they were going to school Wizzy said to Wozzy, 'I've been thinking. I'm going to practise very hard and win the leap-frog race at school.'

Wozzy smiled. 'And who,' he asked, 'is going to be your partner? You can't win a leap-frog race all by yourself, you know!'

'Why, you, of course,' laughed Wizzy.

Wozzy thought for a little while. 'Yes, that would be fun,' he said at last. 'When shall we start practising for it?'

'Right now, of course!' replied Wizzy, and the two little frogs played leap-frog all the way to school.

Mr Toad, the headmaster, was surprised to see them arrive so early for school.

'Good morning, Mr Toad,' they both panted. 'We're practising for the leap-frog race.'

'I'm very glad to hear it,' he remarked. 'I want somebody to help me tidy up the classroom, so you are both just in time!'

Wozzy didn't say a word, but he looked at Wizzy as if to say, 'I don't think your idea is such a good one after all!'

Every day for a whole week Wizzy and Wozzy were first to school and every day for a whole week they tidied the classroom. Mr Toad *was* pleased.

The great day for the leap-frog race arrived, and Wizzy and Wozzy lined up for the start.

'Are you ready?' said Mr Toad. 'GO!' He waved his handkerchief and away they went. In a moment or two, the two little friends were leap-frogging along faster than all the others. Very soon there were only two big frogs in front of them.

Wizzy took a deep breath and leap-frogged better than he had ever done before. They crossed the finishing line and Mr Toad judged them the winners.

When they went up to get the first prize from Mr Toad, Wozzy said to Wizzy, 'That was a jolly good think you had, Wizzy. You'd better have another one.'

Wizzy smiled as he said, 'I'll try.'

Rob and his Wish-Away Tree

Rob was in the park, lying in the grass at the foot of a tall tree. He gazed up and up to the very top, and soon he was imagining that he was way up there in the branches, swaying gently back and forth, *swish swish*, back and forth, *swish swish* . . .

And very soon his eyes were closing and he was thinking, 'I wish, I wish – I wish I were in a tall sailing ship, flying across the open sea . . . I wish, I wish.'

Swish swish came the sound of the waves against the ship. *Woosh woosh* came the salty spray in Rob's face as he looked out from the ship's crow's-nest across the beautiful blue sea. Below him, the deckhands were hard at work.

And what was that on the horizon? Land! they were nearing land at last – he could just make it out.

'Land ahoy,' he shouted down below.

Suddenly, big, heavy clouds moved in and the sky darkened. Rob felt the first drops of rain. *Swoosh swoosh*, he felt the movement of the ship as the waves got bigger, and his eyes grew heavy.

When they opened again, he was no longer in the sailing ship. He was lying in the grass at the foot of his tree and it was beginning to rain. He got up and ran off, and all the way home he was thinking, 'I wonder where my Wish-Away Tree will take me next time.'

Copy cat Genevieve

The female residents of Catnap Village were annoyed. It was time to do something about Miss Genevieve Whiskers – she was turning into a terrible copy cat.

If Jenny Tabby bought a straw hat with flowers one day, Genevieve would go and buy one just like it the next. If Polly Persian had fish cakes for dinner, Genevieve made sure she had them too. If Mirabelle Mousecatcher decided to go on holiday to Trout River, Genevieve went on holiday to Trout River too. It was really very tiresome for everybody.

So, Jenny, Mirabelle and Polly called a meeting of all the lady cats in the village to discuss the problem, and they hit on a clever plan.

The next day was Monday. Genevieve was mildly surprised to see five of her acquaintances in the same hat.

On Tuesday, she was even more surprised to find a group of six lady cats in the fish shop, *all* buying sardines for dinner.

And on Wednesday, she was astonished to hear that half the cats in the village were going on holiday to the same place, they had all chosen Buttermilk Farm.

On Friday, she burst out to Jenny Tabby, 'Why, you're all a lot of boring old copy cats!'

Jenny Tabby just smiled and said, 'If I were you, I wouldn't take any notice of us.'

Genevieve put her nose in the air and replied very firmly, 'You can be sure of that.'

And from that day on, no-one in Catnap Village was ever again heard to call Genevieve Whiskers a copy cat.

The noisy town-hall clock

Dong, dong, dong, the town-hall clock was saying. Everyone looked at their watches in surprise, for surely it was only three o'clock? But the clock went on striking.

Mr Crust the baker ran from his kitchen dusting the flour from his hands. He gazed up, astonished, at the clock. *Dong, dong, dong.*

Mr Brawn the butcher hurried into the square still carrying a string of sausages. *Dong, dong, dong.*

'What's happened to it?' exclaimed Mr Crust.

'Where's Mr Mold the watch repairer?' shouted Mr Brawn.

Mr Crust and Mr Brawn scurried round the town searching for Mr Mold, but no-one had seen him at all.

'This is terrible!' groaned Mr Brawn. 'Come along Mr Crust, you and I will stop that wretched clock.'

So the two went to the clocktower and climbed the stairs until they reached the little clock room at the top. From behind

the door came a dreadful noise–*Dong, dong, dong*–and another noise too. It was someone shouting, 'Let me out, let me out!'

The door was locked but the key was in the lock. Mr Brawn soon had the door open, and inside was poor Mr Mold the watch repairer. At once the clock stopped striking, and the people down in the square gave a big cheer.

'How did you come to be locked in here?' asked Mr Crust, in surprise.

'It was some rascally boys,' shouted Mr Mold angrily. 'They crept up behind me and locked me in, the rogues. I kept making the clock strike hoping someone would come to my rescue. Thank goodness you did!'

Then, suddenly, Mr Mold began to laugh. 'Were you going to stop the clock with those?' he chuckled, pointing to Mr Brawn's hand.

And then they were all laughing together, for Mr Brawn was still carrying a string of sausages.

A few bad boys were sent to bed very early that day, and people in the town never ever forget the day the town-hall clock went wrong!

Tom Trotter stars on stage

Everyone laughed at Tom Trotter. He was such a fat little pig, with a very solemn face, and he was so perfectly sure that he had a beautiful voice.

'You should go along to the Woodland Theatre today, Tom,' said Kitty Cat. 'They want people with good voices to take part in the new play.'

'Do they?' said Tom, feeling very excited. 'That sounds like a good chance for me. I shall probably get a leading part and become famous.'

'Yes,' laughed Reggie Rooster, 'and we'll all come to see your act.'

Of course, Kitty Cat and Reggie were really joking, but Tom went trotting off with great ideas in his head. He put on his best blue suit, and he wore a nice loose collar so that he might sing more easily. He had on his new black shoes with shiny buckles. The shoes weren't really comfortable, and he couldn't walk very easily in them, but they did look smart.

When he got to the theatre Tom was not sure which way to go, but at last he found himself on the stage where Olly Owl was holding auditions.

Tom sat quietly waiting for his turn.

'Very good!' cried Olly Owl, as Ruth Rabbit finished a little song and dance.

'I think you will be excellent for the part of the Princess. Just practise that top note, my dear. Next, please.'

Rover the farm dog sang a song and recited in a very deep voice. He was given the part of the villain in the play.

When Tom Trotter's turn came he felt nervous and excited. 'I'm sure my voice is better than any of those,' he said to himself. 'Oh, I do want to be in the play!'

He walked up to the front of the stage, and he lifted his chins from the loose collar so as to sing his best.

But, oh dear!

'Grunt-unt-nt!' sang Tommy.

'Hahaha!' laughed everyone.

Olly Owl was quite angry. 'I want people with good voices,' he cried. 'Run away, little pig, and don't waste my time!'

Tom's eyes filled with tears. He hadn't got a beautiful voice after all. He turned away sadly.

But the new shoes were pinching him and he had trouble walking properly. One toe caught in a piece of rope and over he went! In fact, he went over and over so many times that all the animals started to clap and cheer.

'Splendid!' cried Olly Owl. 'You are quite an acrobat—just what we want! You shall have the part of the jester in the play. You will not have to sing, but if you can turn somersaults like that you will be a great success.'

So Tom Trotter was the jester in the new play, and he made everyone laugh so much that he decided he would forget all about being a singer, and be a clever acrobat instead.

The Blue Persian

Little Tabby Cat lapped up the saucer of milk that had been put down for his breakfast, stre-e-e-tched, and then wandered out into the sunshine. With a light spring, he landed on the fence between his home and the house next-door.

Yesterday, there had been a lot of hustle and bustle in that house. Jannie, his young mistress, had said some new people were moving in.

'I wonder if the new people have a kitten,' Little Tabby Cat thought.

That very moment, the door of the next house opened, and to his surprise out walked a kitten! But a very strange kitten, Little Tabby Cat thought. Her fur, instead of being short and smooth and striped like his own, was long and silky and a beautiful shade of blue.

'Hello,' said Little Tabby Cat cheerily.

'Good morning,' said the blue kitten haughtily.

'What is your name?' Little Tabby Cat asked.

'Lady Katrina of Ware,' said the blue kitten. 'You can call me Trina if you like. What is your name?'

'Little Tabby Cat,' he said, wishing it sounded grander.

'Is that all?'

Little Tabby Cat nodded, looking rather ashamed.

'And that's what is written on your pedigree?'

'On my *what*?' asked Little Tabby Cat.

'Pedigree. I suppose you *have* a pedigree?'

'I don't even know what a pedigree is,' Little Tabby Cat admitted.

'My pedigree is as long as . . . as long as all your whiskers put end to end. It is a list of the names of my father and mother, and of their parents – and so on, back through many years. They have won hundreds of prizes. I have only won three so far, but I will probably win a lot more when I am grown up.'

'Prizes?' said Little Tabby Cat.

'Yes. At Shows, you know. But there, I suppose you don't go to Shows. You aren't a Blue Persian, are you?'

'Would I win prizes if I were blue?' asked Little Tabby Cat.

'Perhaps,' Trina said. 'I am going to explore my garden now. Goodbye.'

Little Tabby Cat sat on the fence, deep in thought. If only he were blue!

Then he remembered that yesterday Jannie's father had been painting some

He tried to see if there was any paint left. He put up a paw and pulled the tin towards him. Over it went. Yes, there *was* paint in it, and it poured all over Little Tabby Cat, covering him from head to tail. But it wasn't blue paint. It was bright red! He had found the wrong tin.

Mewing miserably, he jumped down from the shelf and ran out of the shed and along to the kitchen door, leaving a trail of red paw-prints behind him.

'Why, Little Tabby Cat!' cried Jannie when she saw him. 'What *have* you been doing?'

She called her mother, who held up her hands in horror at the poor, paint-covered kitten. She fetched some cleaning liquid and shampoo and between them she and Jannie cleaned off all the red paint.

'That's better!' said Jannie. 'Now I can see your pretty striped coat again.'

Little Tabby Cat purred with pleasure. He wasn't a Blue Persian, and he didn't have a pedigree, but Jannie loved him, and that was really all that mattered. Who cared about prizes, anyway?

chairs a beautiful bright blue. Perhaps there was still some paint left in the tin.

He scrambled down from the fence and ran to the shed. The door was open and inside, high on a shelf, was a tin of paint. Little Tabby Cat sprang, and landed right beside the tin.

41

Magellan goes to school

Magellan the mynah bird was perched in the window looking out at the garden and feeling very bored. There was no-one at home to talk to. Annabel was at school and her mother and father were out shopping with Leonard the labrador.

'Oh dear, what a boring old day,' he sighed. But suddenly, his eyes lit up and he fluffed his feathers and chattered to himself: 'I've got an idea, a wonderful idea. I shall go and visit Annabel at school.'

So away he went – out by the kitchen door, down Rose Lane, along Whistler Road, in the school gate, through the classroom window – and FLAPFLAP-FLOOF landed on Annabel's desk.

'Magellan!' exclaimed Annabel in amazement.

'Well done, Annabel,' said Miss Sweetapple the history teacher, who was writing on the blackboard. 'That's exactly the right answer – the name of the Portuguese explorer was Magellan.'

'I thought there was only one Magellan in the world – ME,' came a rather cross voice.

Miss Sweetapple looked round sternly from the blackboard, but when she saw the mynah bird on Annabel's desk, she began to laugh.

'Well,' she said, patting him on the head, 'you may not be the only one in the world, but you're certainly the cleverest Magellan I've ever met. I'm pleased to have you in the class.'

Magellan replied, 'I'm pleased to be here,' and settled down to enjoy the rest of his first day at school.

Turn to pages 12, 67 and 82 for more stories about Magellan the mynah bird.

The new burrow

One day Rob Rabbit made up his mind to dig a new burrow. He chose a nice shady spot and then he sat down to think.

Rob Rabbit hated work. He was such a lazy fellow! But at last he began to scratch the earth away with his front paws.

Every few minutes he sat down for a rest so it was a long, long time before the burrow was done.

'I shall need some grass to make it cosy,' said Rob Rabbit. But the grass was upstairs in the meadow and Rob Rabbit was far too lazy to fetch it.

All of a sudden he saw a hole in the wall where some of the earth had fallen away while he had been digging. On the other side of the hole was another little room. A strange creature was asleep there on a cosy bed of grass.

'I will borrow some of that grass for my warren,' said Rob Rabbit to himself.

Very carefully, Rob Rabbit put his paw through the hole. Then bit by bit he stole the grass. Soon there was just

enough for the strange creature to lie on – no more! Then he filled up the hole again and lined his burrow with grass. It all looked very cosy.

'Now I will find somone to come and admire my burrow,' he said.

The first creature he met was Old Mole who looked very cross.

'Do you like my new burrow?' asked Rob Rabbit. 'I have lined it with grass that I stole from a room next-door, but nobody will ever know.'

'Indeed!' exclaimed Old Mole, looking crosser than ever. 'That was *my* room, Rob Rabbit! I wondered who stole my grass. Now you just come and find me some more.' And he made Rob Rabbit collect lots of grass for a new bed.

Rob Rabbit had no time to be lazy then.

The day Bubble met Squeak

Bubble was a very happy sea-lion. He lived in the zoo in a big pool all by himself, and he never ever felt lonely. He was used to having a chat with his keeper, Fred, twice a day, and in-between fish he would have a quick word with people who came to watch him at feeding-time. And he loved to show off his balancing tricks. The crowds always clapped and cheered and he felt very proud.

So life was pretty good really – until the morning Fred came to tell him that a new sea-lion was coming.

'What?' said Bubble indignantly. 'Someone else in my pool? It won't work.'

Fred's face fell. He thought Bubble would be pleased. 'She's a very nice sea-lion,' he coaxed. 'Her name is Squeak.'

'What a silly name!' replied Bubble. 'No, I just know we won't get on. Anyway, there's not enough room for both of us. She'll be a nuisance.' And with that, he swam to the other end of the pool.

Fred arrived next morning with two other keepers and the new sea-lion. Bubble lounged on the side of his pool, put his nose in the air and looked in the opposite direction.

But what a surprise he had when he stole a glance at the new sea-lion! She was really very beautiful. 'Maybe it won't be so bad after all,' he thought, and with a happy flapping of flippers, he hurried over to her and said hello.

Fred just stood by and sighed, 'Thank heavens for that!'

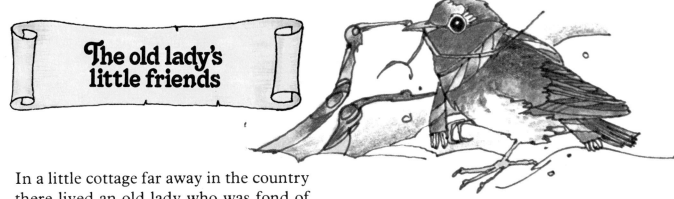

The old lady's little friends

In a little cottage far away in the country there lived an old lady who was fond of the birds. Every day after breakfast she put some crumbs for them on the bird table in the garden.

One morning when the snow lay very thick all around, there were no crumbs on the bird table.

The birds were feeling hungry so the robin flew to the old lady's window and hopped up and down upon the sill.

'Chirrup, chirrup!' he called, tapping on the pane.

The old lady came to the window and opened it. 'I'm sorry little friend, but I have no crumbs for you today,' she said. 'You see, the snow is so deep that I can't walk to the woods to gather sticks for my fire, and without a fire I can't cook the food which gives you the crumbs.'

The robin flew away very sad, but he soon thought of a way to help the old lady who had been kind to him. He flew to every bird in the garden and whispered something in his ear. At once each bird flew off to the wood.

The next morning when the old lady opened her front door she was very surprised, for there on the doorstep was a big heap of sticks that the birds had left for her.

'Chirrup, chirrup!' called all the birds in the garden.

'Oh what kind friends you are!' cried the old lady.

Every time it snowed after that, the birds left sticks on the old lady's doorstep, and every day the old lady put out crumbs for them on their bird table.

'For one good turn deserves another,' chirped the robin.

Our Clara

Clara the cow was a perfect nuisance, or so Farmer McKay thought. She was *always* wandering off on her own. None of the other cows ever did – just our Clara.

It wasn't usually too hard to find her, but this time Farmer McKay was having a bit of trouble. She wasn't in the orchard, she wasn't in the hen-house and she wasn't in the stable with the horses. Where was she then? He searched all the paddocks and went next-door to Farmer Clod, but there was no sign of Clara anywhere.

There the search had to stop, for Farmer McKay was due to take John and Mary and Eliza to the fair in the local village.

It was a wonderful fair and packed with people from miles around. The children were very excited as they ran from the roundabout, to the helter-skelter, to the coconut shy and on to the candy floss stall. But Farmer McKay couldn't stop thinking about Clara. 'Oh well,' he sighed, 'I guess she'll turn up.'

At that very moment, he felt something nudge his arm. He turned round to see what it was and there was our Clara, munching on a toffee apple. Farmer McKay couldn't believe his eyes, but he was very pleased to see her. He gave her a hug and said, 'You're such an adventurer, my girl, I'm surprised you're not sliding down the helter-skelter.'

And as they walked out of the fairground, Clara looked at him with her big dark eyes as if to say, 'I'm not that much of an adventurer. I just like a bit of fun now and again – that's all.'

A doll called Button Nose

Button Nose was a rag doll, and she belonged to Mary. Sometimes she wished that she had another home. Mary had a young dog called Chips and he was very playful. When he felt like a game he would pick Button Nose up in his mouth, carry her around and suddenly drop her to look for a bone instead.

'I'm a very unlucky doll,' thought Button Nose.

Just then, Mary came along and picked Button Nose up and Mary's father came in from the garden with a bowl of strawberries.

'Come and have some, Mary,' he said. 'We'll eat them outside under the trees.'

Mary jumped up, tossed Button Nose down on the sofa and the poor doll started to fall off the back. When Button Nose stopped falling she found herself lying in the dark.

'I'm on the floor behind the sofa,' whimpered Button Nose when she looked around. 'No-one will ever find me here.'

About an hour later, Mary came back inside and started to look for Button Nose. When she couldn't find the doll the little girl began to cry bitterly.

Mary's mother and father helped her search the house but none of them thought of looking behind the sofa. Poor Button Nose–there was nothing she could do.

But suddenly, a small, furry paw came around the end of the sofa. A curious nose began sniffing. The paw stretched further back to the wall. It was Chips.

For the first time in her life, Button Nose felt glad to see his beady eyes looking at her. The next moment she was caught up in his mouth and was carried to Mary.

As she nestled in Mary's arms Button Nose changed her mind about the dog.

'I will never again complain about Chips carrying me around,' she decided. 'If it hadn't been for him I might have stayed behind the sofa for days.'

The magic skipping rope

Jane ran down the garden path to look for her brother Tom, but she stopped when she saw her skipping rope lying on the ground.

The skipping rope was coiled up like a snake and as Jane watched, her eyes grew round with surprise, for the rope slowly uncoiled and began to move down the garden path.

'Mummy!' she cried. 'My skipping rope is magic. It's moving by itself!'

Her mother came running out to the garden and stared in amazement as the skipping rope slithered gracefully down the garden path to an apple tree, where it slowly rose from the ground, swaying from side to side as though in a dance.

'Goodness! It really must be magic,' said Mummy.

Then suddenly, a big red apple fell *plomp* on the ground beside Jane. She looked up and saw Tom in the tree.

Tom climbed down and chuckled with glee. For it was he who had been making the skipping rope move, by pulling it along with a length of black thread.

'Ha, that was a good joke,' he laughed.

'At least it helped me to find you,' said Jane.

'And only just in time,' said Mummy, 'for in another few minutes the icecream we have for tea would have melted away.'

48

There were only two residents of Guinea Pig House. They had their names on a white card which hung just outside the front door. It read 'WOFFLES – Please ring' and, underneath, 'SQUEAKY – Please knock.'

Not that the notice made any difference at all, because Woffles and Squeaky lived together in the same room. It was rather strange too that there was no bell to ring at Guinea Pig House and no knocker to knock with.

Every time Simon, the little boy who kept them, came to bring them their fresh carrot or cabbage leaves Squeaky would say to Woffles, 'We shall have to do something about that bell. I can never hear it.'

'I hear it very well indeed,' replied Woffles, haughtily. 'It's your knocker that never seems to work.'

'We won't argue about it now,' said Squeaky.

'No, don't let's argue,' agreed Woffles. 'Let's listen very hard at tea-time and see if you can hear my bell.'

'Or, you hear my knocker,' put in Squeaky quickly.

Then they both went for an afternoon's nap in the straw and woke up just in time to hear Simon opening the garden shed door.

'This is a silly notice,' they both heard Simon say. 'How can you ring a bell when there's not a bell to ring or knock at a door without a knocker? I must have been playing some game or other when I put that up. I think I'll change it.' And he set to work.

'That'll do,' he said to the guinea pigs who had come out of the straw to watch. 'From now on nobody will ever forget about you,' and he showed them both his new notice: *'Don't forget to feed the guinea pigs.'* Then he stuck it on the front of their house and went away.

Then Woffles sniffed a little and said, 'I was sure I could hear my bell.'

Squeaky nodded, 'And I was sure I heard my knocker,' he replied. 'We must both have been wrong.'

Woffles nodded. 'In a way,' he said, 'I'm rather glad. It always did start an argument. And this notice really means something.'

'It means more and more fresh carrots . . .' began Squeaky.

'And more and more fresh cabbage leaves,' added Woffles.

It did too, and the two guinea pigs never argued about anything again.

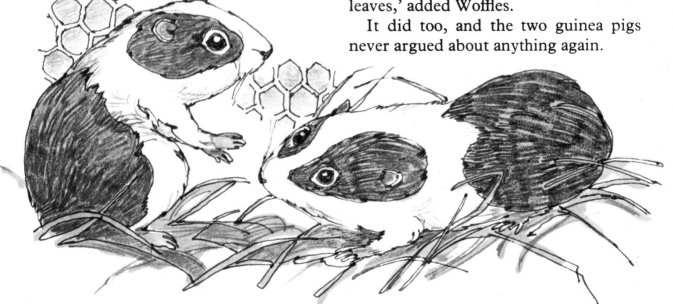

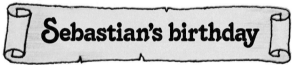

Sebastian's birthday

Sebastian Stoat's birthday was in the winter. It was usually dreadful weather, but he always had a small party. This year, he had invited his friends Bill and Barney Badger over for a meal and a game of snakes-and-ladders.

When Sebastian woke up on the morning of his birthday he could hear the rain pelting down.

'Oh dear,' he thought, 'it's going to be a dreadful day.'

It certainly was – it rained and rained and rained.

'Perhaps they'll decide not to come,' thought Sebastian sadly, thinking of all the food he had prepared. However, he laid the table for six o'clock and made a roaring fire.

Soon there was a knock on the door and with a beaming smile Sebastian

hurried to open it. There stood two dripping figures in rain-coats and wellington boots. They had come after all, and soon they were sitting warmly by the fire and enjoying Sebastian's wonderful feast.

After supper they all helped to clear the table and wash up, and then they settled down to an exciting game of snakes-and-ladders, while the wind howled and the rain poured down outside.

It was Bill Badger who first noticed something creeping underneath the door.

'What's that?' he asked in alarm.

Sebastian got up to have a look and discovered to his horror that the hall was full of water. They were flooded!

'Come on, fellows,' he shouted to his guests. 'Upstairs!'

They scrambled up the stairs in great haste. Sebastian found them some pyjamas and they all squeezed into his

big double bed. They knew they would be safe there till morning and soon they were fast asleep.

First thing in the morning Sebastian, Bill and Barney jumped out of bed and looked out. All they could see was water. Then they looked downstairs – water again.

Soon there was the sound of splashing outside and a voice called, 'Ahoy there! Does someone want rescuing?'

'Yes, please!' shouted the friends from the window.

It was Will Weasel in a boat. 'Can you climb down?' he called.

'Wait a minute,' said Sebastian, as he pulled the sheets off the bed, knotted them together and tied them to the bedpost.

'You first,' he said to Bill.

Bill swung down into the boat, then Barney followed, and last of all came Sebastian.

'Hurrah!' cried the friends, and Will Weasel rowed them away to a little island that had escaped the flood. There Percival Pig showed them to a hall where kind helpers were giving out bowls of steaming soup.

They all sat round the fire and warmed their toes.

'I shan't forget this birthday in a hurry,' declared Sammy.

'Nor shall we!' echoed the badgers, as they tucked into their soup.

wasn't there. All he had in his pocket was a big hole!

'I'm terribly sorry, Mr Miller,' said Tim with a gulp, 'but I won't be able to pay for the sweets.'

'We'll fix that, my boy,' said Mr Miller, giving him a wink. 'Why don't you come back here behind the counter for a little while and help me out, to pay for your sweets.'

Tim's eyes opened wide. 'Oh, that would be stupendous!' he exclaimed, and soon he was busy unpacking boxes of sweets and filling up the storage jars.

Mr Miller was so delighted with Tim's good work that he asked him if he would like to come back and help in the shop another time.

And what do you think Tim's answer might have been?

Tim and the sweetshop

They always got on well together, Tim and Mr Miller the sweetshop owner. Tim called in there now and again when he had some pocket money. He often thought he'd like to be Mr Miller and work in a sweetshop. Mr Miller had a long counter full of the most delicious sweets in the world, Tim thought. There were fruit gums, peppermints, humbugs, chocolate bars, liquorice allsorts, orange chews, fruit bonbons, coconut ice.

'Oh yum,' thought Tim as he made his way along the counter one morning. When he had picked out a bagful of sweets, he asked Mr Miller how much they would be and dug into his pocket for his money. But, oh dear, his money

A new life for an old horse

For ten years Andy trotted up and down the streets pulling Mr Perkin's milk cart. He was a very contented horse. The housewives gave him apples and crusts of bread and the children shouted, 'Hello Andy,' and patted him on the nose.

But one sad day Mr Perkins decided that Andy was too old to pull the milk cart any longer, so he put him into a horse-box and took him into the country to live.

When Andy trotted out of the horse-box into a big empty field he felt very lonely and unhappy. He so wished he was back pulling the milk cart.

Then, suddenly, the village school bell started ringing, and down the lane beside the field scampered a crowd of boys and girls. When they saw Andy standing there in the grass they ran to the gate and leaned over to talk to him.

Andy trotted over to them and felt much happier as they chatted to him and patted his nose. When all the children had gone he munched some of the fresh country grass and then he started to explore his new home, nosing into the hedge and rubbing against the tree in the corner of the field.

It seemed only a little while before the school bell rang again, and the children came running back down the lane. It rang four times that day and every school day. Each time this happened, Andy ran to the gate and the children stopped to pat him.

In a few weeks Andy had lots and lots of new friends who came to see him every day, even in the school holidays. Life in the field wasn't so bad after all. In fact, he thought it was going to be much more fun than pulling that old milk cart.

The fittest rabbit in the village

'I'll show them,' declared Stirling the rabbit as he strode out of the sports shop in Marigold Village with a brown paper parcel under his arm. 'I'm sick of all my friends saying I'm lazy, hrrmph, so there.'

Soon he was admiring himself in his full length mirror – sideways, frontways, any way he looked very fine in his new bright red tracksuit and red and white running shoes. 'In a week's time I shall be the fittest rabbit in the village,' he said importantly, flexing his flabby arm muscles.

Training started bright and early next morning. Stirling jogged along, *pant pant pant*, bravely, *pant pant pant*, through the park, swam at the local pool, sat in the sauna, worked out in the gym, played badminton and jogged home again – all in one day! The village rabbit folk were amazed at his energy.

BUT, when Stirling got home at last, he was exhausted, and he fell thankfully into his comfortable armchair. When he tried to get up he had an awful shock – he was stuck fast! His muscles wouldn't budge!

'Oh,' he called, 'help!' and his neighbours came running. And do you know, they laughed till they cried at the sight of poor Stirling.

'That's more like our lazy Stirling,' they chuckled. 'Settled into his armchair again.'

But they were nice rabbits really, and they did help him up to bed. And all Stirling could say was, 'Who'd like a new red tracksuit? I shan't be needing it ever again.'

Frankie and the night watchman

'Brrr!' shivered Frankie the fire engine. 'It's such a cold night, I think I'll take a little run to warm up my engine.' And he pushed gently at the doors of the fire station until they swung open.

'Now I think I'll go along to where the workmen were mending the road today, and talk to my friend the night watchman. He's sure to have lit a nice hot fire.'

But when Frankie reached the road repairs, he was puzzled. Instead of a bright, warming fire, there were only cold black coals in the old iron bucket. The watchman looked out from his small wooden hut, with a glum face.

'You do look cold, poor man,' said Frankie. 'Why don't you light your fire?'

'I can't,' the watchman shivered. 'I've lost my matches.'

Frankie shone his searchlight but the matches were not to be seen.

'That *is* a funny thing,' said the watchman. 'I know I put them away in a safe place.'

'Look in your pockets,' Frankie suggested.

The watchman turned out his overcoat pockets. He found a few coins, a cheese sandwich, a treacle toffee, and two lengths of string.

The watchman wrinkled his forehead, and thought. He sighed, and took off his hat to scratch his head. And out of his hat fell the box of matches!

'The safe place was too safe,' chuckled Frankie.

The watchman smiled as he lit the fire and the coals glowed red.

'I often put fires *out*,' said Frankie happily, but I've never helped light one before.'

There is another story about Frankie the fire engine on page 24.

The Old Black Engine

The stationmaster told the porter, 'They're going to close the line.'

The porter shouted to the engine driver, 'They're going to close the line.'

And the engine driver whispered to the Old Black Engine, 'They're going to close the line.'

'*Aaaah,*' said the Old Black Engine, and '*Aaaah,*' again.

The engine driver polished his engine so lovingly.

'No more work for you and me, old friend,' he said. That was what he always called his engine – 'old friend'. It was his pet name.

'You will have to stay all day and night in your shed. And I shall have to sit at home and smoke my pipe.'

They were both very sad.

The next week the stationmaster said to the porter, 'Tell the engine driver to clean up the Old Black Engine. Make her look smart for her last trip down the line. I shall be wearing my top hat.'

So the engine driver took his cleaning rags into the shed where the Old Black Engine lived, and got to work.

'We'll give you a good shine all right, old friend,' he whispered, as he polished away with his rags. 'We'll show them.'

There were crowds of people on the platform, all waving flags and shouting, 'Hurrah for the Old Black Engine! Hurrah!'

And so the Old Black Engine started on its last trip down the line. Over the

level crossing, under the road bridge, past Manor Farm and through the Pine Woods it went. At every station people stood on the platform cheering and waving flags. But the engine driver and his old friend were unhappy because they knew this was the last trip of all.

That night, when the engine driver had driven the Old Black Engine back into its shed for the last time, he said 'This is goodbye for you and me, old friend,' and he shut the door of the shed and went back to his home. So the Old Black Engine was left all by itself in the shed. It was all by itself for days and days and months and months.

Then, one day, a gentleman in a bowler hat came to see the stationmaster. This gentleman was carrying a briefcase, with a great many important papers inside. He took out the papers and showed them to the stationmaster.

'Whatever do all these words and numbers mean?' asked the stationmaster.

'Why,' said the gentleman in the bowler hat, 'they mean that you will have to open the line again. I'm afraid we made a mistake. It shouldn't have been closed.'

So the stationmaster told the porter, 'They're going to open the line again!'

The porter went to the engine driver's house, and shouted to him, as he sat in his doorway smoking his pipe, 'They're going to open the line again!'

The engine driver took his cleaning rags out of his drawer, and ran all the way to the shed where the Old Black Engine was living, and polished his old friend until she was beautiful and shiny.

'Aaaah!' said the Old Black Engine.

And the very next day, they set off down the track and everybody was happy to see the Old Black Engine back on the line again.

Too friendly to win races

Young Billy was a fine-looking little boy, with very long legs. He was taller than any of the children in his class at school and he could run much faster. He was also very, very friendly.

When the school's sports day came round in the summer, Billy and his friends Mike and Davey were so excited that they couldn't concentrate in lessons for two days before. The most important event was going to be the running race. They were all in that.

'I'm going to win,' declared Mike. 'I can run really, really fast.'

'I can run faster than you,' said Davey. 'I'll beat you all.'

Billy didn't say anything. He knew he could run faster than either of them, but he didn't like to boast.

On the day, all the children turned out for the races and their parents were there to watch them. Soon it was time for Billy's race and he lined up on the starting line with the other competitors.

CRACK went the starting gun and they were away. Billy got off to a fine start ahead of all the others. In second place were Davey and Mike. Billy ran like the wind but when he glanced over his shoulder and saw that he had left his friends behind, he slowed down to a steady jog – so that they could catch up!

'What a funny little boy!' said his mother who was watching from the sidelines as the three boys crossed the finishing line together.

'No, not really,' chuckled his father. 'He's just too friendly to win races.'

Mrs Brown Hen's babies

Mrs Brown Hen was very worried. She had six little babies all yellow and fluffy like Mrs Speckly Hen's children, but somehow they looked different. Their feet were much larger and they didn't say, 'Cheep, Cheep, Cheep,' but made quite a different sort of noise.

They grew very quickly and Mrs Brown Hen would say, 'Please don't waddle like that. You must learn to walk daintily like this,' and she would lift up each leg very carefully to show her children how to keep their feet nice and clean. But it was no good, they kept on waddling.

Then one day Mrs Brown Hen decided to take her family for a walk across the field. Now in this field was a pond and Mrs Brown Hen said, 'Do be careful, children, or you will fall in and get very wet.'

But to her dismay the six fluffy children waddled straight into the water, making funny quacking noises, and swam around quite happily.

'Oh, please come out at once,' said Mrs Brown Hen, rushing up and down the bank. But they wouldn't.

'Hello, Mrs Brown Hen,' said Peter who had come to sail his boat on the pond. Then he saw the ducklings in the water.

'Oh I see, your babies are swimming and you think they'll drown. Poor Mrs Brown Hen, they are ducklings that you hatched out, not little chickens,' he said.

'So that's why they waddle around and make such funny noises,' clucked Mrs Brown Hen, ruffling her feathers. 'Oh well! I shan't have to worry about them any more,' and she settled down happily to watch them all swimming on the pond.

Chicken for Curlytail Sam

Curlytail Sam was a little pig who simply adored roast chicken. He thought about it all day long.

Now one day, after school, Curlytail Sam decided to go home a different way, past Farmer Snout's farmhouse. When he reached the farm he stopped suddenly and sniffed the air. As well as the usual nice country smells there was another one – a delicious one.

Quietly, Curlytail Sam tiptoed up the path and peeped through the kitchen window and there, pink-faced and jolly, was Mrs Snout, the farmer's wife, roasting a whole row of chickens over the kitchen fire. Curlytail Sam's mouth began to water.

Just then Mrs Snout looked up and saw him, and being a kind and understanding sort of pig, she opened the door and said, 'Come in, little piglet, and tell me why you are looking so longingly through my window.'

So Curlytail Sam came in and told her all about his longing for roast chicken. 'I can't help it,' he sobbed. 'I just keep on thinking about roast chicken all day long.'

'Well, don't cry dear,' said kind Mrs Snout. 'I think I can cure you, but you must do exactly what I tell you.'

Mrs Snout smiled to herself as she put three roast chickens on a dish and said, 'All right, you just sit down and eat these, but mind – you must eat *every single scrap!*'

The chickens were simply delicious. Curlytail Sam gobbled up the first one and enjoyed every bit. The second he ate more slowly as he wasn't feeling very hungry any more. 'I don't think I can eat the other one,' he said.

But Mrs Snout said, 'Now come along, eat them all up. Remember, you promised to eat every single scrap.' And she would not let him go until every bit was eaten up. Poor Curlytail Sam. He felt dreadful.

'Never . . .' he said, as he staggered out of the door.

'NEVER,' he said, as he crawled up the hill, 'will I think of roast chicken again!'

And he never did.

A walk with Uncle William

A circus had arrived in the village, and the twins were able to watch the hustle and bustle from their garden. Hundreds of fairy lights gleamed on the huge tent. Brightly coloured caravans filled the circus ground and the circus folk were busy running here, there and everywhere preparing the horses, elephants, tigers, lions and all the other circus animals for the evening show.

'Oh, it *is* exciting!' Ann cried.

'Can we go to the circus tonight, Mummy?' Johnny asked eagerly.

'I'm afraid you can't go tonight, dears,' his mother replied. 'Uncle William is coming to tea, and you know how he always likes to take you for a long walk after tea.'

'Oh dear, why did Uncle William have to choose today to come to tea?' Ann said.

Soon Uncle William arrived, and the twins followed him indoors.

'Is the tea ready?' asked Uncle William. 'We'll go for our walk soon.'

'Do we really have to go for a walk, Uncle?' asked Johnny, hoping his uncle would say that they needn't go.

To his surprise Uncle William threw back his head and roared with laughter.

'You'll like *this* walk,' he said with a chuckle. 'It's to the circus ground. I bought four tickets for tonight's show.'

Ann and Johnny could hardly believe their ears.

'Oh, how lovely!' they cried. 'We're going to the circus after all!'

61

The cuckoos change places

Henry was a cuckoo who lived in a little house on the wall above old Mrs Willow's china cupboard. The little house was really a clock and all Henry had to do was to pop through the front door every hour and shout 'Cuckoo!' the right number of times. He did it once for one o'clock, twice for two o'clock and so on.

One day, when old Mrs Willow had gone shopping, Henry sat on his door-step feeling rather unhappy. The truth was, he was very tired of shouting 'Cuckoo!' all day, every day, and he wished he could do something else.

Suddenly, far away, he heard a familiar sound. 'Cuckoo!' it went. 'Cuckoo! Cuckoo!'

'It's a cuckoo like me,' said Henry excitedly.

The sound came nearer and soon, onto the window-sill of old Mrs Willow's cottage, flew a cuckoo.

'Hello,' said Henry. 'My name's Henry and this is my house.'

'Hello,' said the other cuckoo. 'My name's George and I live in the woods. What do you do in your house?'

When Henry told him George said enviously, 'How I wish I had a cosy little house like yours.'

'But you have all the world to fly in,' cried Henry.

'Ah yes,' said George, 'but sometimes I'm cold and hungry. Then when winter comes I have a long journey across the sea to find the sun.'

'What fun!' cried Henry. 'Could we change places?'

And George, who had cold feet from

sitting in draughty trees, thought it would be an excellent idea. So they changed places, and Henry flew into the woods and George lived in Henry's house.

But time meant nothing to George. He could never remember when to shout 'Cuckoo!' and when he did he would shout it twice at twelve o'clock, and twelve times at two o'clock.

Old Mrs Willow was very cross with him and took the clock to the clock-mender. The clock-mender rattled it and turned it upside-down. Then he shook his head and said, 'I think it's just old and needs a rest.'

So old Mrs Willow sadly put the clock away in her china cupboard. Poor George was very bored shut up in there all day.

And Henry? He was having an awful time. He could never find enough to eat, and the wind blew his feathers backwards, which annoyed him very much. Soon the weather grew cold and the other cuckoos flew away to find the sun.

'I shall never manage to fly all the way across the sea,' Henry thought unhappily. So he flew back to old Mrs Willow's cottage instead.

'Cuckoo, George,' he shouted. 'Where are you?'

'Here I am,' came the muffled voice of George. 'Do let me out.'

Henry did, and George said, 'Thank goodness! You can have your house and welcome to it.'

And with a joyful 'Cuckoo!' he flew out of the window and disappeared.

Henry popped back into his house and made a great deal of noise opening and shutting his front door to see if it needed oiling. When it came to three o'clock he popped out, exactly on time. He shouted, 'Cuckoo! Cuckoo! Cuckoo!' and then popped in again.

Old Mrs Willow was delighted and put the clock back on the wall, while Henry settled down for an hour's nap, thinking, 'This is the life for me!'

Granny's wish

In the attic of Granny's house was a big box. Nadia called it 'Granny's treasure box', because of the wonderful things there were inside it. It was full of shoes and dresses and hats and lovely materials. Nadia spent hours dressing up in the attic.

One day she thought she would dress up as a Fairy Queen. She put flowers and a paper star in her hair, and made a dress out of pretty pink net.

'But there's still one thing missing,' she said to herself. 'A Fairy Queen must have a magic wand.' So she made a wand of silver paper.

'You look exactly like a Fairy Queen,' said Granny when she saw her.

'Then wish for something,' said Nadia, 'and I will see if my wand will make it come true.'

Granny thought for a while and then she said, 'I wish it were spring.'

'That's a hard one, because it's still winter,' said Nadia. 'But I'll do my best.' And she lifted her wand in the air and waved it three times.

No sooner had she done so, than there was a loud knocking on the front door.

'I'll go,' she said, and ran to answer it.

On the doorstep stood a gipsy selling flowers. 'Would you like a bunch of flowers?' she asked.

'Oh yes please,' cried Nadia and she gave the gipsy a few coins from her money-box. Then, with the bunch of flowers in her hand, she ran back to Granny.

Granny's eyes shone when she saw the present Nadia had brought her.

'Snowdrops!' she said. 'Oh, how lovely! Snowdrops are the very first promise of spring.'

'Then I've made your wish come true,' said Nadia. 'It's spring already!'

A surprise for Mathilda

More than anything else in the world, Mathilda the goat loved food. There were certain things that she specially enjoyed – like blackberries and mushrooms and pink rose petals – but she was always eager to try something new.

So, she made sure that she kept an eye on the vegetable garden. She wasn't allowed in there – it had a high fence all round it and a heavy wooden gate. But she could see what was growing inside, and one day she spied some tasty-looking plants that she hadn't noticed before. Now and again, she would run over to the fence and look to see how they were getting on.

One sunny morning, Mathilda had a lovely surprise, for there, peeping out from among the leaves of her special plants were some bright red fruits.

'Mmmm,' she said, 'they *are* coming along nicely.'

A week went by and she couldn't wait a minute longer. She had to try the bright red fruits.

'What a bit of luck!' she exclaimed as she trotted up to the garden. 'Some kind person has left the gate open for me.' And she slipped joyfully through the gate, over the carrot patch, past the lettuces and plunged in amongst the bright red fruits. CHAMPCHAMPCHAMP.

But then, 'Ooh ah, oooh,' cried Mathilda miserably. 'My mouth is burning up,' and she ran helter-skelter out of the garden and down to the stream for a long, cool drink.

Oh, silly Mathilda. Do you know what she had eaten? Chillies! And chillies are *very* hot!

A windy night story

'*Whooo-ooh*,' went the wind as it blew round Mother Dimple's cottage.

Mother Dimple was in bed with the blankets tucked up tightly to her little red button nose.

'Oh go away wind,' grumbled Mother Dimple crossly.

But the wind wooed and whistled and whined and hurled itself about until Mother Dimple sat up in bed and shook her fists.

'Go away you stupid wind!' she cried. Still the wind blew.

Mother Dimple got out of bed and lit a candle. Then she pushed her feet into woolly slippers and wrapped herself in her big red shawl.

'It's no good, I will never sleep,' she told herself. 'I shall have some hot milk and then perhaps Mr Wind will blow himself away.'

Her kitchen was warm and sleepy, and soon she had a merry blaze in her stove and the milk on to warm. Mother Dimple sat in her big armchair and listened to the noisy wind. But what was that? A sad little crying noise outside in the wind.

The noise came again – small and sad.

Mother Dimple opened her cottage door and there at her feet was a little black kitten. He was very pleased to see Mother Dimple.

Soon they were both sitting by the fire and enjoying the warm milk.

'Bless me, what a hungry little kitty!' she cried, as it lapped up the milk. 'I have always wanted a black kitten,' she said lifting him into her lap. 'I must think of a nice name for you kitty.'

But kitty was fast asleep, and soon Mother Dimple's head began to nod. She was warm and happy, and forgetting all about the wind, she too was soon sound asleep.

A watchdog called Magellan

One sunny Saturday, Annabel and Mummy and Daddy went off for a walk in the park with Leonard the labrador. Leonard loved taking everyone for a walk in the park but Magellan, the family's pet mynah bird, preferred to stay at home. He made a very good watchdog.

Now, there was a young rascal at Annabel's school, called Terrible Tim. He was always up to naughty tricks and scaring the children. But one thing Terrible Tim knew for certain was that he could never scare Leonard the labrador.

So he was very pleased to see Leonard going out for the afternoon with the family. This was the chance he'd been waiting for – the chance to get at those lovely red, juicy apples in Leonard's garden.

Terrible Tim crept stealthily up the lane at the back of the house and peered over the fence. He licked his lips at the sight of the apples, put one foot on top of the fence, sprang up and then ... WOOF WOOF WOOF GGRRRRR, came the very frightening sound of Leonard the labrador.

'Oh no, it must be Leonard back from his walk,' howled Terrible Tim. And with a yell he fell off the fence, bruised his knees and ran away as fast as he could.

Magellan watched him go and, with one last WOOF, hopped off his branch in the apple tree.

Look out for more Magellan the mynah bird stories on pages 12, 42 and 82.

The special chocolate cake

Pixie Pudding Basin's tea parties were a real treat for the inhabitants of Daisy Dell Village. The Pixie produced a new and exciting dish every month – something so very wonderful and delicious, in fact, that it seemed to have been made by magic. Daffodil Dabble Duck always remembered the Melting Moments, and then there was the Flyaway Cake that Fairy Brightwings would never forget, and Croakie Frog's favourite, Jungle Jelly – oh, and there were many more!

But one month, something awful happened. Pixie Pudding Basin ran out of ideas! For days he sat and thought about the party food, but not a single idea came to him. In the end, it was too late to make anything, so, feeling very unhappy, Pixie

Pudding Basin had to go along to the bakery in the next village.

'I want something special for my tea party,' said the Pixie sadly.

'Try this,' beamed the baker, putting a large chocolate cake on the counter.

'Well, it's certainly big enough,' said the Pixie, 'but it doesn't look very special to me. Never mind, I'll take it.'

His guests licked their lips when they saw the cake the next day. But the Pixie felt terrible, because he knew they would be disappointed. What could he say about the cake when he hadn't made it?

As he cut the first slice, he stammered out a few words: 'This is the chocolate cake that . . .' but he didn't finish, for his mouth fell open in surprise. The cake was growing back where he had cut it, and soon it was whole again!

His guests were amazed. 'Hurrah for the Pixie,' they all cried.

The Pixie couldn't believe his eyes, but now he knew what to say about the cake. 'This is the chocolate cake that grows,' he announced triumphantly. Then under his breath he whispered, 'I must ask the baker for his recipe.'

One winter's day

One winter's day when the woods were very lonely and bleak, Little Grey Squirrel sat on a bare branch of an oak tree.

'How cold the world is!' he thought. 'I must find somewhere to hide.'

But there were no cosy leaves on the oak tree to hide among, and he could find no hollow place to snuggle into. If only he had saved some nuts and made his bed ready, instead of chasing Red Squirrel all summer. Anyway, where was Red Squirrel?

Suddenly, as he sat shivering and thinking these things to himself, there was a stir among the mouldering leaves below. Then, to Little Grey Squirrel's amazement, a sharp nose pushed its way through.

Red Squirrel looked up at his little cousin and chuckled softly. 'Hello, Little Grey Squirrel,' he said. 'Are you still awake? Are you going to chase me again?'

Little Grey Squirrel shook his head miserably, but said nothing.

'Silly fellow,' laughed Red Squirrel. Do you know, you were shivering so much that the whole tree wobbled. That is what woke me up. You see, if you looked really closely, you would see that this old tree is hollow. I have a fine, cosy bed here. Why not climb down and share my home with me?' asked Red Squirrel, kindly.

Delightedly, Little Grey Squirrel leapt from his lonely bough and slithered down the trunk. 'Oh, thank you, Red Squirrel,' he said, and he was soon snugly inside.

'How cosy it is here,' he whispered. 'Red Squirrel, I *am* sorry.'

But Red Squirrel was already fast asleep.

'I will tell him in the spring,' thought Little Grey Squirrel, closing his eyes.

PET SHOP

Mick and the rabbits

There was a little white rabbit in the pet shop in town and Mick liked it so much that he asked his parents if he could have it for a pet.

'We'll see,' said his father, but that usually meant no.

Mick went off to bed feeling disappointed, but he cheered up at the thought of the next day at school. His class were to have an Easter egg hunt. Chocolate eggs would be hidden in the school garden.

Miss Davis, the teacher, called all the children together the following day and told them that the Easter eggs were rather special this year, so to look out for something different.

Then the hunt was on. The children ran noisily to and fro looking for the eggs,

but Mick stood very quietly by the sandpit. He couldn't believe his eyes, for there sitting up in the sand was a brown rabbit! It sat perfectly still. Mick went closer. 'Gosh,' he murmured, 'it's a chocolate rabbit. Not quite the same as a real one,' he said, thinking of the little white rabbit in the pet shop, 'but nice anyway.' And he ran all the way home with it that afternoon to show his mother and father.

They had something to show him, too. In the garden stood a rabbit hutch, and inside sat the little white rabbit.

'A brown rabbit and a white rabbit, all in one day,' chuckled his father, as Mick hugged his new pet to him.

The little lost bird flies home

It may sound strange but sometimes you can be lost and yet be quite happy. It was like that with the little bird in the wood.

'This is lovely,' he said to a passing bird, as he perched on a branch.

The other bird looked at him. 'Go home, you silly thing,' he tweet-tweeted.

Then the little lost bird remembered that he couldn't go home, because he didn't know where he lived.

'Where is my home?' he asked.

'Try the open fields,' came the reply.

'All right,' promised the lost bird. He was soon perched on a hedge and asking a hare with long ears where his home was.

'I don't know, little bird,' said the hare, 'but I should try the town.'

But it was worse still in the town. There the sparrows pecked at the little lost bird and drove him away.

'Go home,' they chattered. 'Go home.'

The unhappy little bird flew up to the church tower.

'Ding-dong-ding-dong!' Suddenly all the bells in the tower pealed out. 'Ding-dong-ding-dong! Your home is far away. Over the wall and down the lane. Ding-dong! Across the fields of growing corn.'

So, the little lost bird flew on until he came to a farm. The cows were coming home to be milked and called out to him, 'Hello. So it's you at last. Moo, moo!'

'Yes, indeed,' twittered the lost bird, 'it's me, all right, but who am I?'

'Ask at the farmhouse,' grunted some pigs.

So the bird flew on until it came to the farmhouse. It was a friendly house with a green door and he could hear someone crying. Then the little bird knew.

'Don't cry,' he chirped as he made for an open window.

'Mummy!' cried a happy little girl. 'Mummy! It's my bird. He's home.'

The bird saw his yellow cage and hopped inside and then he sang a beautiful song to say how good it was to be home again.

Mr Mole sweeps the chimney

Mr Mole was cold – brrrrr! Winter had come, and it was time he had his warm fire going again.

He found some dry wood and some matches, and very soon there was a splutter . . . and a puff . . . and the fire was alight. But what was this? Mr Mole put on his glasses to take a closer look. Something was wrong! The smoke came out into his cosy little room instead of going up the chimney.

'Oh dear me!' he coughed and choked. 'This will never do. I must let the fire go out and tomorrow I will sweep the chimney.'

Mr Mole went to bed cold and rather miserable, but next morning he got up early, determined to get the chimney swept straightaway.

'First of all,' he said, looking very workmanlike in his bright blue overalls, 'I must find a brush to sweep with.'

He went outside and searched among the trees in the wood. 'Perfect! Just the thing,' he cried, picking up a small branch from the fir tree.

He trotted back into his house and pushed the branch as hard as he could up the chimney.

'This–is–hard–work,' he puffed, 'but–it–should–soon–be–through–the–top.' And sure enough it was, but someone else had spotted it – Mr Magpie!

'Ha–ha,' chuckled Mr Magpie. 'I think I might give Mr Mole a helping hand.'

And the naughty bird got hold of the end of the branch which was sticking through the top of the chimney and *pulled*.

Now, that would not have mattered quite so much if poor Mr Mole had not

still been holding on to the other end. As Mr Magpie pulled, so Mr Mole slid up into the chimney with the branch.

'There, I'm sure it's clean now,' laughed Mr Magpie and letting go of the branch, he flew away home. *Whoosh–splutter–flop*! Into the hearth fell Mr Mole, all covered in soot.

Just then came a knock at the door.

'Oh Mole, you do look funny,' said Mr Badger, doubling up with laughter.

For one moment Mr Mole didn't know what to do, but then he too burst out laughing.

'Now to work to clean up this mess,' said Mr Badger.

He disappeared, but was back in no time at all with Sid Squirrel and Hop and Skip, the rabbit twins.

'Don't worry, we'll help you,' said the little squirrel.

'Yes, we will,' agreed the twins.

So they put on their little aprons and sorted out dusters and tins of polish, then everyone set to work. Mr Mole carried away the soot, Sid Squirrel brushed down the walls with his bushy tail, Mr Badger cleaned the floor and shook the rugs, and the twins polished the furniture until it shone. When they had finished, the room was sparkling.

'Now, you must all stay with me and we'll have a party,' said Mr Mole happily, as he lit his fire.

After they had eaten as much as they could, they all sat round the blazing fire toasting their toes, and Mr Mole told them how pleased he was that they had come along to help him that morning. As they settled down into their chairs they all agreed dreamily that it had been well worth it.

Roberto's first painting

Roberto the bear was rather pleased with himself. He had a brand new easel and he was setting it up to begin work on his very first painting.

'Roberto the artist – yes, a grand name for one as talented as I. Now, what shall I paint?'

He took off his new navy blue beret and scratched his head. 'A house? No. Some flowers? No. A sunset? No. Oh dear, I can't think of anything – this is terrible. Perhaps I could begin with a spot or two of black in the middle of the canvas.'

So he stepped up to the easel with his palette in one hand and his brush in the other and dabbed three little spots of black paint on the canvas. But what next? He heaved a sigh. It wasn't so easy being Roberto the artist, after all.

Just then, his friend Rupert came along. 'I'll help,' he said, and taking up the palette and brush, he began to paint. A dab of red, some patches of brown, a smudge of navy blue, a few black lines, and the painting was finished.

'Why, it's a picture of me!' cried Roberto happily.

He kept the painting, but he thought that Rupert should have the new easel. After all, Rupert was just as good a name for an artist as Roberto.

The umbrella

Soon, they came to an old beech tree. 'Look up there,' cried Robbie, pointing to an overhanging branch.

There was a rustling of leaves, and then Smoky sprang from the tree, and landed almost at Sally's feet. Robbie picked up the kitten, and they all squeezed underneath the big umbrella.

'It's getting rather crowded under here,' laughed Sally.

Just then, the rain stopped. As Sally closed the big umbrella, she knocked Robbie's cap from his head.

'Hey!' he cried, as the breeze whisked the cap into the middle of Farmer Brown's duck pond.

'Oh dear!' cried Sally, but suddenly she had an idea. She fished out Robbie's cap with the handle of the umbrella.

'I say,' said Robbie, as they walked on up the lane, 'that umbrella's jolly useful, isn't it.'

'Yes,' answered Sally with a smile. 'Now I understand why Granny called it her best friend.'

'Put on your raincoat if you go out looking for Smoky,' said Sally's mother.

Sally was standing beside the open door, watching the rain and wondering where her kitten was.

'Can I take Granny's old umbrella instead?' asked Sally.

'Old umbrella indeed!' said Granny, handing it to her with a smile. 'That umbrella is my best friend.'

'Smoky, Smoky,' called Sally as she went outside, but there was no sign of the kitten.

Then Sally saw her brother Robbie, running up the lane.

'Robbie, have you seen Smoky down there?' she asked.

'I'm not sure,' panted Robbie, ducking underneath the big umbrella. 'I saw a cat in one of the trees – I'll go back with you if you like!'

A little boy's birthday treat

The little roundabout was very tired. His painted animals had been going up and down, round and round, all day and he felt hot and grumpy.

'I'm going to have a rest,' he said to himself, as he slowed down.

'Hop on! Hold tight!' said Mr Jones to the children as he took their money. Then he tried to start the roundabout. He pushed, he pulled, he looked inside the little roundabout. He took off his hat and scratched his head.

'That's funny,' he muttered. 'I can't find anything wrong with it.'

'Everybody off!' he shouted. 'The roundabout won't start.' Then he gave the people their money back.

'Maybe it's too hot,' thought Mr Jones. 'I'll let it have a rest,' and he went away to have his tea.

Soon everyone else had gone away, too, except for one little boy. He still stood there with his mother. Tears were running down his cheeks.

'Let's go home,' said his mother. 'We'll come back again tomorrow.'

'Tomorrow's not my birthday—it's *today*,' sobbed the little boy.

The roundabout began to feel unhappy too. 'I might be able to go just once more,' he thought, 'to make the little boy happy on his birthday.'

Presently, Mr Jones came back from tea. Seeing the little boy standing there, he said, 'I'll try again.'

He turned the handle. With a tired little squeak the roundabout started up.

'All aboard!' shouted Mr Jones.

The little boy climbed up. He was laughing now. The roundabout forgot his tiredness as he gave his passenger a birthday treat. And Mr Jones stood quietly in the middle shaking his head in wonder.

'It's almost time to start work,' said the sweeping brush.

'Is that why you are looking so happy?' asked his friend, the mop.

'Ah, yes,' the sweeping brush replied. 'I'm always happy when I'm working.'

Just then, Mrs Merry came bustling into the kitchen, and taking the sweeping brush from the cupboard, she carried him to the dining-room. Sweep, sweep, sweep, he went.

'You are a good sweeping brush,' said Mrs Merry.

But suddenly, a terrible thing happened. Mrs Merry's gold ring slipped from her finger onto the floor and with one stroke, the sweeping brush had swept the ring down a mouse hole!

Mrs Merry peered and prodded in the mouse hole, but try as she would, she couldn't get the ring back.

'You don't look very happy now,' said the mop, as Mrs Merry carried the sweeping brush back to the cupboard.

But the sweeping brush had an idea. The next day, when Mrs Merry fetched him to sweep the dining-room, he swept as before. Sweep, sweep, sweep, he went, but this time he left just a few crumbs lying on the floor, outside the mouse hole.

'What have you been up to?' asked the mop, when the brush came back.

'You'll see in the morning,' the sweeping brush replied.

In the morning, sure enough, there was Mrs Merry's ring – outside the mouse hole. The mice had pushed the ring out of the hole in their eagerness to get to the crumbs, just as the sweeping brush had hoped.

So sweep, sweep, sweep, he went, until he swept the ring up.

'Why, what a clever sweeping brush you are!' cried Mrs Merry. And the sweeping brush felt happier than ever before.

Cosmo's beautiful tail

There was once a kite, called Cosmo, with a handsome red and yellow tail. He never stopped boasting about it to the other kites.

'Just look at my tail,' he kept saying.

'We're tired of looking at your tail, Cosmo,' they said. 'Please go away.'

'All right,' said Cosmo, 'I will, and I'll show the world my tail.'

So one windy day, Cosmo snapped his string and flew happily away into the clouds. Very soon two jackdaws came flying along. Now jackdaws collect bright things, and when they saw Cosmo's tail they were delighted.

'What a splendid tail you have, Mr Kite!' they said. 'Could you spare a piece for our collection?'

'Certainly not,' said Cosmo. But the jackdaws took no notice, and swooping down they nipped a large piece off the end of his tail.

The kite was most upset. 'Oh my tail,' he moaned as he flew on.

Next he noticed some bees making honey in a tree.

'I have the longest, brightest, most beautiful tail in the world,' he called. 'Just look at it!'

'Whatever for?' said a large bee. 'Can't you see that we are busy? Get out of our way, or you will be stung.'

And then, just as Cosmo was escaping from the bees, the wind, who had a cold, sneezed: '*Aaaaatishoo*!'

It blew Cosmo into a tree, so that his tail was torn by the branches, and yet another piece had gone.

Then it started to rain, and the wind, who was still having trouble with his cold, sneezed again, much harder: '*Aaaaaaatishooooo*!'

'Goodness!' gasped Cosmo. 'What's happening?' He flew in all directions until he landed on top of a blackberry bush. Something tugged at his tail. It was a mouse.

'That tail is the longest, brightest, most beautiful tail in the world,' sobbed Cosmo. 'Leave it alone!'

'Your tail is not handsome any more,' squeaked the mouse. 'It would be just nice for lining my nest,' and in a moment he had scampered off, dragging the last piece of tail behind him.

Poor Cosmo was sad. Suddenly the wind sneezed again. The largest sneeze of all: '*Aaaaaaaaaatishoooooo .*'

It blew Cosmo off the blackberry bush right back to the roof-top of the house where he lived.

'Oh, I am glad to be home!' he thought. Then he remembered that he couldn't fly without a tail.

'Why are you so sad?' asked a large black crow perched on a chimney-pot.

'I want to fly down into the garden of this house, but I can't, because I have no tail,' gulped Cosmo.

'I will take you,' said the crow, and he picked up the sad kite in his beak and dropped him in the garden.

'You are very kind,' said Cosmo. 'Thank you very much.'

Cosmo was found the next morning and given a new tail – a tail that was even longer, brighter and more beautiful than the first. But he didn't boast about this one at all.

79

The Waddle Ducks go exploring

The Waddle Ducks were bored with life on Strawberry Farm. They wanted to find an exciting new place to live.

'Come with me, my pet,' said Waddle Drake to Waddle Duck one fine day, 'over the hill and down the lane and we'll see what we can find.'

So they set off side by side.

And they waddled along.

And they waddled along.

And they waddled along until they reached the crossroads at the end of the lane. In the middle of the crossroads was a big sign pointing four ways.

Waddle Duck read the names aloud: '*Strawberry Farm.*'

'We're not going back there,' said Waddle Drake firmly.

'*Clover Hill.*'

'Mmmm, now that sounds delightful.'

'*Muddy Pond.*'

'That sounds even better, my pet.'

'*And Snail Stream.*'

'That sounds best of all!'

'Let's try all three,' suggested Waddle Duck. Waddle Drake agreed and they went off down the road to Clover Hill.

But, oh dear, poor Waddle Ducks! There was no sign of clover at Clover Hill. There was only one tiny puddle at Muddy Pond. And they couldn't find a single snail at Snail Stream!

'I'm going home to Strawberry Farm,' declared Waddle Drake crossly, and Waddle Duck followed.

And when they got there, it seemed like heaven – there was fresh clover to eat, a lovely muddy pond to dabble in and snails to eat as well.

And the last thing Waddle Drake said as he settled down that night was, 'I'm staying right here on Strawberry Farm forever, my pet.'

80

Piglet learns to squeal

What a noise there was coming from the pigsty! Mother Pig was snorting and grunting and her ten little piglets were squealing loudly and rolling about on the straw. All except one wee piglet who was sitting miserably in a corner of the sty.

He was unhappy because he couldn't squeal like his brothers and sisters.

He made up his mind to find a squeal from somewhere, so as soon as the door of the sty was open he slipped out.

First he met Minnie the sheep.

'Please tell me how I can find a squeal, dear sheep.'

'Try munching grass like I do and it

will make you strong enough to squeal.'

So Piglet tried his hardest but he didn't like the taste much.

He wandered on to the chicken-run to have a word with Hetty Hen.

'Please tell me how I can find a squeal, dear hen,' he asked.

'Come and help me peck up this corn to make you grow.' Piglet watched Hetty pecking up the corn with short sharp jabs of her beak, but when he tried he either bumped his poor snout hard or blew the corn away with his snuffling.

He turned sadly away. He would never find a squeal this way.

Suddenly, Hetty and the other hens began to make a terrific noise and dashed round the hen-run. Good gracious, it was a fox!

Luckily, the farmer had seen the fox too and he snatched up his gun and fired. The noise of the gun firing was so loud that poor Piglet jumped high in the air with fright. He ran as fast as his little legs would carry him back to his sty and when he stopped he realised he was squealing!

'Well it took a fox to do it, but I'm a real pig now,' said Piglet proudly. And he went on squealing just for the fun of it.

Magellan orders double icecreams

Annabel and Mummy and Daddy were on their way back from a picnic in the country. Annabel sat in the back of the car with Leonard the labrador, and Magellan the mynah bird perched quietly on the seat beside her. He wasn't feeling very talkative after such a lovely day.

'We must stop somewhere and buy some food for dinner, dear,' said Mummy, so Daddy pulled in at the next shopping centre.

Magellan kept very quiet while the family went shopping. Annabel carried him so that he wouldn't get lost in the crowd.

Their last stop was the delicatessen. 'Ooh, I'd love an icecream,' thought Annabel. 'Mummy, could I have an icecream?' and Leonard went WOOF and Magellan looked interested.

'No dear, you've had plenty to eat today.'

'Ohh,' sighed Annabel.

'Hmph,' grumbled Leonard.

Mummy bought some milk and bread at the delicatessen.

'Anything else, madam?' asked the assistant.

'Yes please,' came a voice just like Mummy's. 'Three double icecreams – two chocolate and one strawberry, thanks.'

'You've done it again, Magellan,' laughed Mummy, and she bought five double icecreams, one for each of them.

You can read more stories about Magellan the mynah bird on pages 12, 42 and 67.

Learning to swim

Mother Otter had tried all day to persuade her little son to swim in the river, but he wouldn't because he was afraid.

'You *must* learn to swim,' she scolded. 'How can you become a proper otter unless you do?'

It was beautifully clear water there in the river, and dragonflies danced above it like tiny rainbows. Little Otter loved to watch them. He liked to look at his own face in the river too. But he would not learn to swim.

Mother Otter was wise and soon she had an idea.

'Come, Little Otter,' she said. 'We must make our home somewhere else. If you will not swim, then you can't become a proper otter. And if you are not to be an otter, you have no business living in an otter's hole by the river.'

Mother Otter found an old rabbit's burrow, but it was hot and stuffy, and their next-door neighbour was a mole who scratched and kept them both awake.

'There is no water to look at my face in,' said Little Otter. 'And, Mother, where are the dragonflies?'

'They are flying on the river where the proper otters live,' said Mother Otter, wisely. 'Here you must be content to watch worms, Little Otter.'

Soon he began to long for the river. 'Mother,' he said, 'we aren't rabbits are we? We are otters! Please may I be a proper otter and learn to swim?'

'Certainly, Little Otter,' smiled Mother Otter. 'But you must be brave.'

'Will you hold me very tight the first time?' asked Little Otter.

'Of course I will,' said Mother Otter. 'And the second time, too. But the third time you must swim by yourself.'

Mother Otter kept her word, and before you could say 'dragonfly', there was Little Otter swimming like a fish!

The mean old dog

All the neighbourhood dogs had terrible trouble with Gruff the bulldog, who lived at number 34 Mill Lane. He was the grumpiest, growliest, meanest old dog they had ever met. He had never, in all the time he had been at number 34, said a polite word to any of them. It was time, said the dogs, to do something about Gruff, so they called a meeting.

Sausage the dachshund was in charge. 'The aim of our meeting,' he said seriously, 'is to find a way of making Gruff a more pleasant dog to live with. Have you any ideas?'

George the Cairn Terrier had one. 'Why don't we all go and jump on him.'

'No, no, no,' groaned Sausage, 'that wouldn't help. What we need is something to quieten him down.'

So they all sat and thought . . . and thought . . . until Alfred the beagle announced, 'I've go it – music!'

'Music?' cried all the dogs.

'Yes, music,' replied Alfred. 'It will calm his nerves,' and he produced an old radio that he'd found down the alley.

All the dogs followed him to Gruff's place. Gruff was there at the gate, snarling as usual. But as soon as the music began, his scowl changed to a dreamy smile, his growl to a sweet hum and, sinking down, he fell fast asleep.

The dogs all tiptoed away, but they were back next morning to meet the new Gruff. He was quiet and relaxed, and a pleasure to talk to – but Alfred carried the radio with him, just in case.

Nothing to do

Fannymaggy leaned over the garden gate and looked down the road.

Her real name was Elizabeth Frances Margaret, but everyone called her Fannymaggy.

The postman came along on his bicycle and rang his bell loudly.

'Hello Fannymaggy,' he called cheerily. 'What are you doing?'

'I have nothing to do,' said the little girl.

'Oh,' said the postman, 'someone's cross this morning,' and he rode away.

Just then Grandpa came along.

'Hello, Fannymaggy,' he said, giving her a big kiss. 'What are you doing this morning?'

'I have nothing to do, Grandpa,' said poor Fannymaggy, with a big sigh.

'That's good,' said Grandpa, 'then you can help me pick up all the apples that have fallen from the trees, and put them in this basket.'

Fannymaggy ran backwards and forwards, picking up all the apples she could find. When the basket was full Grandpa said, 'I'm going to write a big notice and I want you to colour it for me.'

So Fannymaggy brought him her crayons and he wrote some letters on a piece of cardboard: 'PLEASE TAKE SOME'. Fannymaggy went over them with her brightest colours.

'That does look nice,' said Grandpa, when she had finished. And he fixed the notice to the apples and put the basket by the front gate.

'Why are you putting the apples there, Grandpa?' asked Fannymaggy.

'Well, my love,' said Grandpa, 'there must be lots of people who haven't got any apples, so I thought they might like some of ours.'

'What a good idea!' said Fannymaggy.

Later in the morning the baker's boy came by, read the notice and took some apples.

When he saw Fannymaggy watching him he called out, 'Thank you, Fannymaggy.' And several other people did the same.

Mummy came back from shopping.

'Have you had a nice morning, Fannymaggy?' she asked.

'Oh yes,' replied Fannymaggy with a smile, 'and it was all because I had nothing to do.'

A bunch of primroses

'Do take this lovely bunch of primroses to Granny, Little Stoat,' said Mother Stoat one spring day. 'She has been so sick, and they will cheer her up.'

'All right, Mummy,' said Little Stoat. And he put on his best brown cap and set off whistling through the wood.

'What fine primroses, Little Stoat!' said Old Mr Weasel.

Little Stoat nodded politely, and raised his best brown cap.

'Yes, sir,' said he. 'They are for my Granny, who has been very sick.'

'That is a kind thought, to be sure,' said old Mr Weasel. 'I have a friend who has been sick, too. But alas! I have no flowers to take for a gift.'

Little Stoat was very sorry to hear it.

'Please have a few of mine, sir,' he said. 'My Granny won't mind.'

And he carefully plucked a handful of bright primroses from his bunch and gave them to Mr Weasel. The nice old gentleman thanked him and hobbled away by another path.

Further on, Little Stoat met Mrs Badger, who also admired the primroses.

'They are for my Granny, who has been very sick,' said Little Stoat, politely raising his best brown cap.

'Are they, now?' said Mrs Badger. 'I have a dear friend who has been sick, too. I wish I had some flowers to take her.'

Little Stoat was most sorry to hear it.

'Please have a few of mine, ma'am,' he said. 'My Granny won't mind.'

And he plucked a few more of the lovely primroses from his bunch and gave them to Mrs Badger. The good lady wept with gratitude, and hurried away by another path.

Now, on his journey Little Stoat met Tawny Owl, old Grandfather Water Rat, and Mrs Otter–and they all admired the primroses and said how sorry they were that they had no flowers to take to their sick friends. And each time, Little Stoat raised his best brown cap politely and plucked some more of the pretty primroses from his bunch. In the end there was not one primrose left.

Poor Little Stoat! What was he to do?

At first he thought it would be a good idea to pick some more primroses. But they were very hard to come by, for it was rather late in the season.

Next he thought he would pick some yellow daffodils that he found beneath a hawthorn tree. But they looked so cosy and comfortable there that Little Stoat hadn't the heart to pick them.

So in the end he hurried off to his Granny's to explain what had happened.

When he got to Granny's house in the wood he *was* surprised! There was Granny standing by the door, and there were roses in her cheeks because she was so happy. And standing in a straight line were old Mr Weasel, Mrs Badger, Tawny Owl, Grandfather Water Rat and Mrs Otter. They had all come to pay their respects, and each had brought the primroses that Little Stoat had given them.

Little Stoat hadn't guessed that they were all old friends of his Granny.

So Granny had her bunch of lovely primroses after all!

Young Joe Mouse and the cat

Mrs Mouse was busy cooking and cleaning and baking one day when Young Joe Mouse came into the kitchen.

'What can I do, Mother?' asked Young Joe. 'I have nothing to do.'

'Dear me,' said his mother, 'a lovely big house to live in, all your toys, and you can't find anything to do?'

'What are you baking, Mother?' asked Young Joe.

'I'm baking a cheese pudding,' said his mother. 'First I find a basin, then I find the cheese grater to grate the cheese–here it is. Now I get the cheese–oh dear! I have no cheese left. Young Joe, you can run to the larder and fetch me some cheese. But mind, you must watch out for the cat.'

Young Joe had never been out of the hole before, and had never even seen the cat, so he said to his mother:

'How shall I know that it's the cat, Mother?'

'You can tell it by its fur,' said Mrs Mouse.

So away scampered Young Joe to get some cheese for his mother. Very quietly he scuttled along the hall and peeped over the top of Mrs Mouse's front door. But oh, there, right beside the door, was THE CAT! He knew it was the cat because it was a large heap of black fur.

He ran back to his mother. Mrs Mouse

was surprised when he burst open the kitchen door.

'Oh, Mother, Mother!' squeaked Young Joe Mouse, in a very frightened voice. 'The cat is right outside our front door! Come and look!'

Very quietly, they crept along the hall to the front door. Carefully, carefully, Mrs Mouse opened the door.

'Oh, you silly little mouse,' she said. 'That's not the cat. That's a pair of old fur gloves.'

Young Joe laughed. His mother kissed him and said, 'You can always tell the cat by its whiskers. Now away you go.'

So once again Young Joe set off on his errand. This time he got as far as the kitchen fireplace, when: 'ROAR! ROAR!' came a terrible noise. He looked up, and there above him, so big, so high, was – THE CAT! It must be the cat this time because it had so much greyish-white fur, and it had whiskers!

'Ha!' said the cat. 'A little mouse!' And when Young Joe heard the cat speak, he ran and ran until suddenly–*bump*–he ran right into his mother who had come to look for him.

'Oh, Mother,' he squeaked. 'I saw the cat, I saw the cat! It had fur and whiskers and it spoke!'

'Why, you silly little mouse,' said his mother. 'That wasn't the cat. That was Grandpa asleep by the fire!'

So, feeling happy and brave again, he scuttled away for the third time. And this time he ran straight to the larder and back to his mother in no time at all.

'Brave little mouse,' said his mother. 'Now we can have a lovely cheese pudding for dinner.'

Young Joe was very proud and pleased. No-one could say that *he* was afraid of cats.

Presents for the bears

Little Bear had a problem. It was all right for his brother, Paws, he thought. Paws was a big bear now, and he would know what to give Mummy and Daddy and him, Little Bear, for Christmas.

'But I can't think what to get,' sighed Little Bear. 'Oh, ho hum,' and he thought until he was so confused that he ran off to see Mrs Cluck the hen.

'I know just the thing for your Mum,' said Mrs Cluck comfortingly, and with a *cluck cluck cluck*, she produced a smooth

white egg from beneath her feathers. 'Paint a pretty picture on the shell, and your Mum will have a treasure.'

Hazel the horse was helpful too. She found him a very special present for his Dad. 'A horseshoe – give it a polish and it will bring him luck.'

'And now for Paws,' puzzled Little Bear. But the bees reminded him that there was one thing that Paws really loved – honey! 'Put it in a big, round pot and he'll have the best present of his life.'

That night, Little Bear got busy. He painted a pretty picture on the egg, polished the horseshoe and put the honey in a big, round pot.

'Oh, what a treasure!' exclaimed Mummy on Christmas morning when she opened her present.

'It's my lucky day,' said Daddy, when he saw the horseshoe.

'Mmmthisisthebestpresentofmylife,' mumbled Paws, his mouth all gummed up with honey.

'Oh, what it is to have friends at Christmas!' thought Little Bear.

Jessica's Fancy Dress Parade

Just then Uncle Jack came in.

'I know the very thing,' he said.

'What is it?' asked Jessica.

'I won't tell you yet,' he answered, 'but be at my house in plenty of time on the day of the Garden Fête, and I'll have it all ready for you.'

Jessica was at Uncle Jack's house very early on the important day. 'Where's my costume, Uncle Jack?' she asked.

'There it is', said her uncle pointing to a pile of newspapers.

'But I can't dress up in those!' she cried.

'Yes you can. Come along.'

He made her a funny pleated dress out of newspapers, and a smart little newspaper hat. Then he hung a placard round her neck. It read: 'IN THE NEWS.'

'I really am "In the News", aren't I?' giggled Jessica.

Everyone laughed when they saw her in the Parade and she won First Prize. It was a beautiful box of chocolates which she shared with Uncle Jack because, after all, it was his idea.

There was to be a Fancy Dress Parade at the Garden Fête and Jessica badly wanted to enter. But she couldn't think what to dress up as.

Mummy tried to help. 'Be a fairy,' she said.

'No,' said Jessica. 'Jill Anderson is going to be a fairy.'

'Be a pirate,' suggested Daddy.

'No,' replied Jessica. 'Peter Wilson is going to be a pirate.'

'What about going as a shepherdess,' suggested Granny. 'You can borrow Grandpa's walking stick for a crook.'

'Er—no,' said Jessica. 'Daphne is going to be a milkmaid, and they are nearly the same, aren't they?'

Daisy to the rescue

'Just fancy having feet like that,' laughed Sal Kitten, pointing her dainty paw at Daisy Duck.

'When she walks you can hear her all over the farmyard,' giggled Sissy Kitten. 'Flip-flop, flip-flop, flip-flop!'

'Walks?' tittered Sal Kitten. 'Nobody could walk with feet like that, Sissy. That's why she waddles.'

Daisy Duck didn't like the two kittens laughing at her. After all, she couldn't *help* having big, flat feet. But because the kittens were very young and foolish she forgave them.

But the two kittens were very naughty and copied Daisy's funny walk, waddling along in a line in front of her. Then they fell in a heap with laughter.

'Come on,' said Sal Kitten, when she had licked herself tidy again. 'I've found a boat.'

Sal showed her sister Sissy the tin basin that Mrs Farmer had thrown away.

'Ooooh! What a lovely boat!' said Sissy.

'Let's go for a sail on the pond,' said Sal.

So they pulled the old tin basin to the pond and scrambled in. Very soon the breeze was blowing them gently across the pond.

'Hurray! This is lovely,' squealed the kittens.

The old tin basin slowly turned round and round, and bobbed about on the little waves until they reached the very middle of the pond, and then – bump . . . *crash*! The old tin basin had hit a big stone under the water and the kittens had very nearly fallen out.

But now something dreadful was happening. The big stone had knocked a hole

in the old basin and the water was coming in.

'Help!' mewed the kittens both together. 'Oh, help!'

Daisy Duck was hunting for worms in the mud.

'I'm coming,' she quacked, when she saw what was happening, and in no time at all she had swum to the middle of the pond.

'Climb onto my back,' she said to the scared kittens, 'and take care to hold on tight.'

By this time the old tin basin was half full of water and the kittens' paws were getting very wet. How grateful they were when Daisy had carried them safely back to dry land.

'Thank you for saving us, Daisy,' said the kittens humbly.

'We are sorry we were rude to you,' said Sal.

'We will never be rude again,' said Sissy.

And while the little kittens busied themselves drying their paws, Daisy overheard them saying to each other, 'Just fancy being able to swim like that,' and 'How gracefully, too!' and 'Think how useful it would be to have feet like Daisy's.'

And Daisy Duck smiled, quacked softly and went on hunting for worms in the mud.